The Red Scarf

THE
SEAGULL
LIBRARY OF
FRENCH
LITERATURE

The Red Scarf

FOLLOWED BY

Two Stages
and
Additional Notes

YVES BONNEFOY

CENTENARY EDITION

Translated by
STEPHEN ROMER

LONDON NEW YORK CALCUTTA

www.bibliofrance.in

The work is published with the support of the
Publication Assistance Programmes of the Institut français

Seagull Books, 2023

L'Echarpe Rouge © Mercure de France, 2016

Deux scènes et notes conjointes © Éditions Galilée, 2009

First published in English translation by Seagull Books, 2020
English translation © Stephen Romer, 2020

ISBN 978 1 8030 9 294 2

British Library Cataloguing-in-Publication Data
A catalogue record for this book is available from the British Library

Typeset by Seagull Books, Calcutta, India
Printed and bound by WordsWorth India, New Delhi, India

For Mathilde

Contents

The Red Scarf

An 'Idea for a Story'

Here I am, in front of a folder that contains my successive drafts for an old 'idea for a story'. So where is it, this folder? It has remained for many years in a little desk, made by my maternal grandfather with his own hands, a piece of furniture fashioned from cheap wood, simple in form, upon which he would place his papers, cover them with his small, dense writing, and then lift the lid and store his pages beneath it. The upper part of the desk, above the lid, consists of two drawers, each side of a curved, central hollow above which, concealed by a high rim, is a shelf. The lower part, under the lid, is simply a storage space, held up by the four bare legs of the desk. On the shelf, my grandfather would store his pen-holders, which would be perched on little stands made out of wood, sometimes along with his rulers and compasses, for besides being a schoolteacher and secretary to the town hall, he would offer his services as the local land surveyor. Directly in front of him, in the hollow beneath the shelf, he would keep his inkwells, one of blue glass and square, with a narrow neck and stopper, the other round and yellow, of terracotta. Next to the inkwells lay the blotting paper and a slide rule, made of fine ivory, lying in its case of pale wood. In the drawers to the side, there is a stash of rubber stamps, boxes of drawing pins and erasers that I have never touched. When

I inherited this lowly desk from my mother, the hardened erasers and the stamps were still inside, throughout the entire time she possessed it, and I have never had the heart to part with them.

Underneath the lid, however, where my ancestor kept the books that he wrote for his own amusement only, which he would bind up in card or imitation leather, of these, none are there today, for I keep elsewhere the ones that came down to me. In their place I have stored photographs of paintings as well as the file entitled *The Red Scarf*.

This folder is in yellow card, with a ribbon of the same colour to fasten it, and it contains a collection of notebooks and different-sized papers, written in with different inks, because I have used over the years, pens of every description, and different inks, and sometimes pencil. A long series of starts and stops, that has continued, I now see, from 1964. Something endlessly interrupted, and impossible to finish, apparently.

And yet, early on, I had no doubt that I would complete, and in good time, the 'idea for a story' that had come to me. My confidence was such that shortly after having the idea, which I'd immediately called *The Red Scarf*, I felt able to offer the text I was about to write to Gaëtan Picon: it was to be for one of the forthcoming *Cahiers* of the new Mercure de France, a publishing venture we were both running at that time. Gaëtan duly advertised it, if I remember rightly, on the back of one or two numbers of the review, as one of the 'forthcoming' texts . During those same months and with the same confidence, I hatched the idea of an edition to be illustrated by Claude Garache, who'd even started to work on the etchings.

But nothing came of these promises, that were undoubtedly rash, and they led to a prolonged attempt vainly continued, fresh starts followed by long interruptions, that went on for more than forty-five years. For I could not in fact resign myself to leaving *The Red Scarf* unfinished, nor could I leave unresolved the enigma posed by this source of inspiration that had dried up so quickly. I felt that there resided in this casket without a key something significant concerning my thoughts about poetry and my own life. Two or three months before my little book *Two Stages and Additional Notes* came out in 2009, I had once again taken up these pages, still with the thought that I would finish by comprehending what had to be the end of *The Red Scarf.*

II

What I had at my disposal originally, from the earliest days, was a poem of around a hundred lines. The idea for my story would consist of words carried, if not in fact produced, by the exigencies of a rhythm. But when I realized that I did not understand the whole idea for my story, I thought I would resign myself to writing in prose, thereby removing that obstacle. I think I must have argued with myself that the liberties prose affords to linger over thoughts that poetry neglects in its imperious, headlong movements would allow me to notice details that would in turn unlock useful discoveries. But alas, these pages in prose were also useless. I tried to develop the characters I had invented, but I lacked all conviction. One by one I erased these random attempts, sometimes I destroyed them, and all they taught me was that to the original version, written out at a single sitting, I could add nothing.

And no more could I change anything. What had surfaced in these phrases charged with obscure allusions and the appearances of meaning and memories were anxieties that had the solidity of fact, even if I could not place them within my own self, even if they had left a definite trace. The poem—if that is what it was—was not just the start of a thought, open to development, but a text that existed entire, to the last comma; a text I had no right to alter, as if it were the work of another. As if someone within me, but unknown to me, had produced it. And there was no possibility, I had to accept this, that the ideas conceived on the level of consciousness, which came later, could ever find their way into *The Red Scarf.*

III

It is because I was so convinced of this, that in July 2009, after yet another failure, I resolved to never open the folder again, indeed, the desire to destroy it tempted me increasingly. . . . But before I recount what happened a little after, I must reproduce for the reader the pages that were gifted to me on that first day. Here then is *The Red Scarf*. It is constituted of two or three sets of verses that I shall name as fragments. This is the first:

This man, elderly now.
Let me put my things in order, he urges himself,
Let me throw out these school diaries,
The letters from classmates,
From my friends, and girlfriends from student days,
And even these notebooks. He opens one of them,
It contains notes he made in his twentieth year.
'In the museum, this morning,
I saw *Danaë and the Shower of Gold*',
'And so he heard an horn blow'
And: 'knight of the two swords ye must have ado'.
He knows where these words come from,
He remembers the day he read them
And they flash across and dazzle
His eyes so many years after.
He goes on turning the pages.

Further on
'They call me the hyacinth girl.'

And now he finds
An envelope, empty but sealed.
He turns it over,
Someone has written a name, an address,
It is at Toulouse,

Words scribbled over the page,
Throw that out too, he exclaims,
But he doesn't, no, he remembers,
He sees, it is a distant memory,
A man, encountered only once
In an old house, never seen again,

When he was about twenty-five years old.
The walls were whitewashed, what a release
For someone coming from those poor rooms
With their flowery wallpaper!
They had talked,
He can see him in the window recess,
The wall is thick, and behind him
Is the evening light.
Throw away this memory, he insists,
But something he's afraid of
Prevents him.
For that memory, is actually like the negative
Of a photograph in black and white,
Nothing is visible except, from one angle,
This shape that seems born of this night,
And yet
The man there, leaning forwards,
Wears across his shoulders, a red scarf.

So write! Just do it,
However absurd it may be

After all these years,
Write to the address at Toulouse.
Fifty years on, he reasons,
And with just the address of a hotel,
The letter will be sent back to me
And I shall think no more about it.
And what should he write? Something like:
What has become of you? I have not forgotten you.
When you can, send me some news.
He shrugs his shoulders, posts the letter.
It is not sent back.
Weeks pass.

And then one morning,
The same handwriting, more or less,
The same name, the same address on the back,
A reply: You have not forgotten me?
I, too, remember
I can even see you
In that big house, near a window,
In the deep recess.
Why we were there, I no longer know.
Who was with us, I dare not think,
But this has remained in my memory,
Around us everything was grey, night was falling,
But what a contrast! In the gloom
The large red scarf you were wearing!
The memory has returned to me at moments of my life.

The fear is back, but stronger!
A shudder,
The terror born of a footstep
Sounding through an empty house.

Leave,
Take the first train for Toulouse,
Realize that behind
This memory is concealed another,
There is a girl, yes, does she not enter
The room where soon it will be dark,
Does she not hold in her hands, ah but why,
A scarf, does she not say . . .

The ellipses are not in the original text, but I have added
them to indicate the great interruption, which I believe took
place at that very moment. Other than the lines I have just
cited there are, in fact, two further fragments in my folder—
very close to the earliest pages and possibly written on the
same day—that were dictated and not willed, a surprise and
not something imagined; but neither of them extend beyond
the tidal barrier, so to speak, which interrupted the flux of
the original piece of writing.

One of the other fragments indeed follows almost word
for word that original dictation, and I might refrain from
saying much about it, except that at one point of the variant
it is as though I myself entered the scene, alongside the
'the man, elderly now', which turns the latter into a friend

perhaps, or in any case a being I consider to be real, even in the context of a fiction: a nuance that is of some significance. But most importantly this page contains two entirely new thoughts, one of which seems to be directed towards that future I know nothing of, while the other seems rather to deepen the mystery.

I shall therefore transcribe this second fragment too, except for the first stanza that is identical to the first seventeen lines of the original version, as if the reference to Danaë and to the medieval narrative made a kind of common denominator from which the rest would follow. So here is the second stanza and all of the rest. The allusion to the 'hyacinth girl' and even the idea of the envelope has gone: it goes straight on to the discovery of the unknown person's address.

> And he is held up by a name, by an address
> That a hand not his own
> Has written across the whole page.
> A man's name,
> An address of a hotel in Toulouse.
> He thinks about it,
> Yes, that must be when I spent a few days
> That year
> In the village near Toulouse.
> Throw that away too.
>
> But he postpones doing so.
> He ceases wanting to throw anything at all away.

Why does the name linger in his mind?
And what is this shadow of a memory
That seems to take form?
Like the negative of a bad photograph,
One that was over-exposed,
On paper almost completely black,
One can make out just a silhouette,
Someone still young, a man, very thin,
Leaning slightly forwards, towards whom?
In the deep recess of a window.
Is that all? No, because this photograph
Is not a straightforward image, it is
Something almost frightening.
The photo is indeed in black and white,
Yet the man in it, who is speaking,
Wears draped across his shoulders a red scarf.

The next day, he tells me,
I wrote to the address in the notebook.
Fifty years on, I thought,
With just the address of a hotel,
The letter would be returned to me
And I would think no more of it.

So what did I write? Something like:
What has become of you? I have not forgotten you.
When you can, send me some news.
I shrugged my shoulders, posting my letter.
But it did not come back.

And suddenly,
Three weeks later,
The same handwriting, more or less,
The same name, the same address on the back,
A reply: I have not forgotten you either,
Says the stranger. I can even see you
In that big house, near a window,
In the deep recess.
Why we were there, I no longer know.
Who was with us, I dare not think,
But this has remained in my memory,
Around us everything was grey, night was falling,
But what a contrast! In the gloom
The large red scarf you were wearing!
The memory has returned to me at moments of my life.

It was then that my friend was afraid.
A great shudder ran through me, he told me.
The kind of fear born of a footstep
Sounding in a house you know to be empty.

And I left.
I could have tried to telephone,
To call that hotel,
But a memory was beginning to emerge
Still very indistinct.
I remembered the village near Toulouse,
And the house of the young painter

Whom I knew then, briefly,
Then he died. An old house
With deep recessed windows,
With whitewashed walls. And I had drunk
Eagerly, at that cup of whiteness,
I who came from the poor rooms
With their flowery wallpaper.

And so it was that one day
A visitor had come from Toulouse.
Who he was, what he looked like, I no longer know,
Nor what he said; but surfacing
Through my forgetfulness of all those years
Is the feeling I felt at the time,
Hostility and fascination,
It is dark when he tells me all this.
He leans forward to light the lamp.
He straightens up with it between his hands,
He holds it so close that the red of the lampshade
Streams upon his chest.
I think of your fear, I told him.

Listen, he says,
Another memory returns,
I am crossing a bridge,
Holding something in a brownish bag,
Where am I, in what town,
The river flows swiftly, it seems to swell

By the minute, is there
Another bank on the far side? And what might be
These shadows drawing near, so tightly
Pressed one against the other, in the rain
That is now falling? I open the bag,
It contains a mask from New Guinea.
Like a crescent moon.
I just purchased it from an antiquarian,
But that too frightens me,
And I rush to return it the next morning.

And he tells me that he left, yes, left.
I listen to him. The train quits Paris,
Moving out between bare, greyish walls,
Above them, invisible, growls the lightning,
Birds knock suddenly against the windows,
First there are shadows, then the scream.
He goes from side to side in the carriage,
Shadows jostle him, laughing,
He does not know if it is night, or day,
Nor where these stretches of black rock are leading
Or these tunnels with their loud vaults
That waken ancient fears within him,
But he passes through these thresholds, and others, others,
Sometimes as if he is crawling in the mud.
Night, underneath what he thought was day.
My friend

Goes into this inky night, his memory.
Close by him, squatting, and scribbling down.

. . . at which point the fragment ends, except that I know
I was very tempted to add to the pages on which this memory is 'scribbling down' lines that never ceased to haunt me
since the day I discovered them, well before I imagined writing *The Red Scarf*. As soon as I read them, I knew that these
lines were meant for me, rising up from the depths of my
life. They came to me from one of Guido Cavalcanti's great
poems, and here they are, in their place, I like to think,
within my 'idea for a story':

> *Ah, Vanne a Tolosa, ballatetta mia,*
> *Ed entre quetamente a la Dorata:*
> *Ed ivi chiama che, per cortesia*
> *D'alcuna bella donna, sia menata*
> *Dinanzi a quella di cui t'ho pregata;*
> *E s'elle ti riceve,*
> *Dille con voce leve:*
> *'Per merzé vegno a voi'.*[1]

---

1 The first of these two fragments comes from Guido Cavalcanti's *Ballate*
VIII. In *Sonnets and Ballete of Guido Cavalcanti* (1912), Ezra Pound renders them thus: ' "Speed Ballatet" unto Tolosa city / And go in softly 'neath
the golden roof / And there cry out, "Will courtesy or pity / Of any most
fair lady, put to proof / Lead me to her with whom is my behoof?" / Then
if thou get *her* choice, / Say, with a lowered voice / "It is *thy* grace I seek
here" '.

Which was followed, in a way that I found overwhelming:

Questo cor mi fu morto
Poi che'n Tolosa fui.[2]

IV

But now for the other sequence, the third fragment, the one that tried to establish itself on the other side of the obstacle, on which I continued to stumble throughout the years that followed.

In fact, I knew very well that this time I was trying to invent rather than simply to transcribe a message. And I also had the presentiment that the ability to invent was precisely what was to be imminently, and lastingly, denied me. And yet I was obliged to write the beginning of this new chapter. For what else could my hero do, having arrived at Toulouse in the small hours, other than rush to the hotel associated with my mysterious correspondent, ask for him at reception, go straight in and knock on his door? Yes, but what then? Who might the stranger be? What would they have to say to each other, what events might transpire that could match the feverish anticipation of the visitor? As I consulted my imagination, it had nothing to tell me, except that the man I had to imagine or to meet was ill, possibly dying, and that it

2 And the second fragment from Cavalcanti—I include the preceding line, for clarity: 'For the wound I bear within me / And this heart of mine has slain me. / I was in Toulouse lately.'

would be a woman who opened the door to his room. But write I did, and in verse. With my eyes closed, so to speak:

> He knocks at the door, she opens. Ah, aghast
> The expression on the face of this woman.
> You, she cries out, you! But a wall collapses
> Between her and him. Or else is it the night bird
> Who strikes their faces with its wings.
> He has gone
> Since yesterday, my husband has gone,
> We are everywhere seeking for him, but nothing,
>   nowhere,
> Perhaps he is dead.
>
> And he, newly arrived: I recognize you, he says.
> I know you. But she is not listening.

She is not listening. Those are the last words I was able to write, while everything in me was crying out to find out more, apart from a few more lines that came to me, but entirely different, rather as the lines from Cavalcanti had done at the end of the other fragment. These were lines 'by me', this time, apparently unconnected to the other eleven, except for the idea of an arrival, a confrontation.

Here then are these lines, too. Which are the last I find among these drafts: they remained there when, next to the others already quoted; everything I tried consequently to invent, to fit into my story, had as little worth as the sentences one scribbles, the word is apt, during the night, in the dark, when one attempts to capture the fragment of a dream. I wrote, not I think without making one or two allusions to the first fragment:

It is as if Balin arrived
At the drawbridge and blew on his horn.
And his brother is there to face him, his double.
They will fight to the death.

And the combat will go on unceasingly,
The two warriors have dismounted,
Seeking the throat with their swords,
Their blood flows into the grass, night falls.
Now they are on their knees, they stab each other,
Ah, my brother, but why, why?
They collapse against each other, on each other,
Pierced with the same metal.

Balin, and his brother Balan! So the knight 'of the two swords' makes another appearance, after I evoked him in the very first lines of *The Red Scarf*!

I evoked him, but at the time I should have tried harder to understand him, for it might have helped me progress more swiftly with my 'idea for a story'. Of the latter, what struck me the most overall, was my perception of the colour red where nothing of such, absolutely nothing, ought to have been possible in the depths of a black-and-white photographic plate:

something supernatural was at work therefore, the sign of a transcendence. And I had come to think that I would not pierce the mystery, nor understand why, in simultaneous and contradictory fashion, two beings for whom the red was substantially a scarf should each have seen the other wearing it.

Nor did I understand why a knight out of the Arthurian Tales—the one who delivered the 'dolorous stroke', that laid waste the land—should be associated with this phantasm, any more than the woman who appeared, and disappeared, in such distress—or just afraid?—on a secondary level of an enigma already so opaque. And what was I to make of the mask from New Guinea? And why should all of this be obscurely directed towards Toulouse, where I had never set foot, although the *Tolosa*, obviously a mirage in the mind of a Tuscan poet of the *dolce stil nuovo*, stirred me so intensely? Soon enough I realized there was little to gain from trying to fathom *The Red Scarf*, and in the years that followed I returned to it only because those sealed doors ahead of me continued to fascinate, doors from a world as mysterious as a dream, whether of ivory or of horn I knew not.

V

One thing needs to be clarified, however, before closing this first chapter: I am now persuaded that at the time I sought to bring these enigmas to light, I did not really wish to do so. For there existed within me someone who dreamt—a guilty dream, certainly—that a level of reality existed other than the one in which we ordinarily work and think: and from this other place in the mind I hoped to receive messages from time to time, which would necessarily be obscure, if not indeed entirely impenetrable. And there is great pleasure to be gained, when one is so minded, to think that one has discovered such a message, hidden in the sands of our ordinary existence!

So the red in the black and white might after all be the signature of that elsewhere which appears and then vanishes. And as for Knight Balin, who appears and reappears in the three fragments, might he not be one of those masked faces that the metaphysical *imaginaire* stores, with good reason, to keep them hidden away, in the mirror-depths of our condition as exiles?

Ambeyrac

I

In the summer of 2009 I had thus almost decided to abandon *The Red Scarf.* I was even prepared to tear up the bundle of pages, and so clear out the space under the lid of the little desk upon which my grandfather used to write.

But in April of the previous year I had written the narrative that I called *Two Stages.*[3] It had come to me easily. I had given myself up to the kind of writing that arises from the subconscious as much as the unconscious mind, and while those pages were obscure to me, this time there was nothing about them to unsettle me. Further, when I came to correct the proofs for the Italian edition of the text, several of the enigmas seemed to be dissolved, in a way that seemed to me benevolent.

This text did not contain the kind of discoveries that reveal desires or needs that had gone unrecognized and that leave the subject with the task with little besides drawing conclusions for the future that psychoanalysis might suggest. There was something of that, in the brief narrative, but there were also clues that struck me as decisive concerning the original impulse behind my poetic project. From where the text had led me, to stand below a balcony in a palazzo in Genoa,

3 See p. 161.

supposedly real but in fact built up of a montage of memories and symbolic clues, I could see, or rather recall the 'scene', which had given shape to, and nearly torn apart, my poetic vocation. I became aware of the paths it had followed, and understood better the obstacles in its way.

Less apparent, however, was the meaning of another balcony that my dream-narrative had seen fit to raise opposite the first in the courtyard of the beautiful architecture of that house: a balcony on which the same sequence of events seemed to take place, but somewhat delayed . . . Certainly, there was much that remained to be elucidated in *Two Stages*, but at least I seemed to possess some clues, of the type entirely lacking in *The Red Scarf*. And in the spring of 2009 I undertook to investigate the matter more deeply in two 'additional notes' to my narrative; the first one for the Italian volume, the second for the French edition that was published the following autumn. They involved a work of reflection and of anamnesis, that should have alerted me, at the very moment I was about to abandon *The Red Scarf*, to the possibility that the old text, its mystery still intact, must have its place in the perspective opened up by the recent text, and clearly based upon events in my own life.

But still I did not make the connection. In the months that followed, the need I felt, expressed as a title for one of the 'additional notes',[4] must have intensified, for one day as

4 See 'First Additional Note: An Aid to Understanding', p. 166.

I was rereading—why though? I rarely reread my own writings—'An Aid to Understanding' in the French edition of the book, a remark I'd made there suddenly brought to mind something from *The Red Scarf*.

What I noticed was that Toulouse, one of the enigmas in *The Red Scarf*, was present in *Two Stages* in a way that was of equal, though inverse, significance. In 'An Aid to Understanding', Toulouse is never mentioned. But its absence was in fact its presence, even an essential presence, for everything in the narrative attested to the fact that Toulouse had been one of the poles of my thought—or, rather, of my dream—when I was a child.

What happened in the 'note' concerned, in that preliminary anamnesis? Reflecting on the Italian cities I had lived in or visited as an adult, I realized that I had made of them, if not exactly myths, then the crucible from where representations of the world and touchstones of taste emerged and took on almost mythical status: they were readings of what I saw there, assuredly, but profoundly refashioned by the metaphysical *imaginaire*. I had lived these cities, Florence notably, then Rome, and even Venice, as one writes poems, fixated by an idea of life, forgetful of its harsh and chastening complexity, or simplicity; and so I had to free myself from them in the way that poetry, reaching beyond us, has the capacity to deliver us from our phantasms which are merely its erratic wanderings. Which is why I had thought it fitting to set against these dream capitals the great 'resounding' port of

Genoa, whose openness to all needs and goods seems to place it beyond any fixed notion of what ought to be.

But did Genoa, or the Genoa that I then proposed as a model, really constitute a return to the world of things as they are, perceived this time in their own finitude? I suspected not, when I had to reread those pages, so apparent was my own pleasure in evoking colours, sounds, smells, changing forms of light, reflecting water, intensely and gathered all together as only certain painters set out to do. This Genoa *à la* Claude Lorrain or Joseph Vernet was no longer perhaps a crucible of metaphysical speculation, but under my pen it was still an image, a beautiful image, captured at the very moment when I should have pledged myself to what that *réalité rugueuse*—rugged reality—impugns in such complacent evocations.

So nothing was really resolved. The child who dreamt of a reality in essence superior to his own, accessible via the unknown language of his parents—this being the central experience of *Two Stages*—had simply been transposed in my exegesis into metaphysical reading of Italy, ending with a partial acknowledgment of its mirage-like nature, more by its displacement into other places of the mind rather than its total dispersal. And why had there not been in 'An Aid to Understanding'—in which I retrace my origins—a single mention of a certain other great city that had held sway over my child's imagination, the first to have signified an absolute?

The Occitan language of my parents, that I made in mirage the language of the *vrai pays*, or the 'true country', has a capital: it is Toulouse. I shall soon have cause to relate to what point that was true for them. And opposed to Tours, the town of my everyday life and further afield than Toirac, where I'd spent my summer holidays but all the same, just a mere village—was Toulouse, an idea of Toulouse, that had in fact been the haven of my thoughts: from which it follows that I should at least have asked the question in the 'Additional Notes', conferring upon it in my account the same sort of status enjoyed by Florence or Rome—or Genoa—places I had made the springboard of my obscure hope and expectation.

And since I had not breathed a word about it, should I not conclude that there was still matter I had not thought through, or had even refused, in that long explanatory text, long enough perhaps to drown rather than to illuminate what it sought to comprehend? I remarked this, and it was then that I recalled that Toulouse, absent in this text was present in *The Red Scarf*, insistently, and mysteriously. This could not be simply accidental. Indeed, as soon as I realized this, numerous other thoughts came to me, singularly agitating in nature.

I must start with a question. Were the two narratives not in fact complementary; *The Red Scarf* waiting for *Two Stages* to shed light on it, because time needed to pass in my own life, with some accrual of knowledge or experience? Perhaps after all, armed with this key, Toulouse, I would be able to open up the sealed text, as long as I changed course. It was no longer to be a question of completing a narrative left in suspense, but rather of listening to what it said about me, in the pages that were already written.

And following hot upon this discovery, is another great discovery, which I shall unveil here, but whose unravelling in detail will require the whole of the present essay. Toulouse, in *The Red Scarf*? It is because this 'idea for a story' bears upon my own existence, and the relationship with my parents. And the man in Toulouse, who left his address on an empty envelope, to someone who remembers, is none other than my father, speaking to me: for 'this man, elderly now' is none other than myself, desiring to put his past in order. As for the red scarf that he and I see draped over each other's breast, it is what unites us, in a way both invisible and essential, it is paternity and filiation, it is the blood-tie.

It was then that I remembered the red marks I had seen on my father's body during the final months of his life, when medical treatment of the time, still somewhat medieval, prescribed horrible leeches to draw out excess blood. There were undoubtedly further memories to be recovered and understood, within the closed waters of *The Red Scarf*. And this was the task I had now to undertake, following the prompts in the poem, including its allusions to works of poetry or painting, designed possibly as much to prevent my remembering as to preserve my past. So great is the desire to forget, when we know that human reality can exist only in and by means of memory, so long as it frees itself from the phantasms that disfigure it.

II

My most troubling memory, when I was between ten and twelve years old, concerns my father, and my anxiety about his silence.

It was a silence that contained no hostility towards the family. There seemed to be no repression of something that could have been said. Rather, it was the sign that he had given up communicating, or perhaps even thinking, about some question that was nevertheless essential to him.

It was not even anything specially striking that might have been embarrassing or unsettling. Not completely mute, just very few words. And I who noticed it—I was probably the only one who did—wanted to think, and with justification, that he was naturally taciturn, and little inclined to return from his long hours at work—that in any case made talking difficult due to the noise, if not the racket, of the workshop—to a more relaxed, or even playful atmosphere, also one extremely unfamiliar to someone from his origins and milieu. Elie came from peasant stock, between Cantal and the Lot, and I knew that he was from the harsh country of the *causse*, the limestone plateau with its monotonous landscape of bushes and rocks duplicated by the drudgery of the working day—how it is so steeped in silence, that one could start to echo it and come to like it. To which we must add the silence imposed upon him during his years in the army, serving under the burdensome colours of the time. Reserved as I knew him to be, he could scarcely have contributed to parlour talk. Silence is the resource of those who recognize, if only unconsciously, the nobility in language.

And then there was his tiredness that came on early, and his illness, the diabetes caused by bad diet, abnormal blood sugar levels, and the heart wearing out. I had witnessed with alarm the first and very unexpected signs; for example on that Sunday afternoon, on a rare visit to the cinema, when he had had to leave right in the middle: it was 1931, and at the very same instant, '*Actualités*' was showing tanks and soldiers half-lost in a black mist—the invasion of Manchuria by the Japanese. A greast wave reared up and crashed over us two years later when we moved house, supposedly to a better area, a little house replacing the humble lodgings of the earlier years; in practice it meant my father had to walk considerably further to get to work. He did this four times a day. Taking the same direction as that of the Lycée, which I'd started to attend that year, I would see him move off, or return, slowly and painfully, walking along the boulevard, an avenue of large chestnut trees and bourgeois houses.

So there are many reasons that might explain his silence. And nothing about it to suggest that it was a way of being noticed or a provocation. At home Elie seemed content to work in the garden, hoeing, sowing and watering the six or eight beds allotted him by the owner of the place, who lived on the floor above us. He spent his summer evenings and his Sunday mornings in the garden. And when the moment came for the Sunday walk, he wore a stiff-collared white shirt, gaiters over his shoes, pale gloves, a soft hat and even a cane. And so it was, disguised as a petit-bourgeois, that he would obligingly come along with us, although most often a step or two ahead or behind the others.

There was solitude, in his silence. And I think I realized early on that I must understand his way of leading, or of losing, his life and at the same time ask questions about the woman, still young, who shared so much with him, in the kind of intimacy strengthened by worrying about money and how to make ends meet.

III

There did in fact exist between my father and my mother substantial differences that might have been a cause of misunderstanding or disappointment. They were born into different social milieus, with differences of upbringing and education at home and in the classroom. Hélène was born in the middle Valley of the Lot, between Carjac and Conques, where the villages were not really poor. In one of them, Ambeyrac, on the Aveyron side of the river, her father, Auguste Maury, was the teacher I have already mentioned: he was an intellectual, in his own modest way, someone who would have liked to read more and participate more widely than the constraints of his life allowed. He had nevertheless made an effort to better his condition. Born the illegitimate child of a shepherdess from the high plateau, who kept a herd of pigs under the little oak trees, he should by rights have been a farmworker or a soldier; the new republic, however, required that the mother should send him to school, and he enjoyed it, applied himself and came first in the district School Certificate, which enabled him to progress further along a path his village knew nothing of: to another school, with a grant this time, and thence to the Ecole Normale at Rodez, where they trained teachers.

It was at Ambeyrac that he spent the greater part of his career. Adhering devotedly to the lay religion of the State, whose creed was progress, with its clear and simple values and its strict but convincing moral code, he spent his evenings and his holidays writing the books I mentioned above, apparently with no intention other than to satisfy his curiosity and keep his intelligence alert. He wrote a moral treatise, a history of France, a collection of anecdotes, a drawing manual and several other works that he never sought to publish, but which he must have shown to his daughters, Lucie and Hélène, who were also his pupils in the single class at the school attended by children from the neighbouring farms. My mother remembered these classmates, numbering about ten or fifteen, with great affection. Their families, who knew each other and exactly what everyone was up to, in a world that for them never changed, formed a society that was more or less atheist, or even peaceably pagan; where the priest demanded no more than token observance, and where the little boys and girls ran through the fields, trying to smoke maize leaves and singing songs in the local patois. It was a paradise, said Hélène, speaking of that time. Setting aside the fine dresses and the ribbon in the hair, the games, songs, kisses and bouquets were almost out of Baudelaire's poem 'Moesta et errabunda' (Grieving and Wandering).

After primary school at Ambeyrac, my mother was set to go to the college at Villefranche-de-Rouergue, but then, at thirteen or fourteen, a sudden illness, a combination of meningitis and typhoid, changed the course of her life. For several days Hélène hung between life and death, and one evening she heard the doctor, who thought she was unconscious, say on leaving the room, 'She won't last the night.' She survived, however, though she remained very weak for several months, and could not progress as far along the path leading to her father's profession as her elder sister did, and this caused her a lot of distress. The teacher, sure that she knew he would be disappointed by her failure, devoted himself to her elder sister. He never spoke to her again in the same way.

Out of hurt pride and sorrow, she decided to exacerbate the row that was brewing, left her teacher training and set upon becoming a nurse. There was at that time in Bordeaux, the first of its kind in France, a hospital that was also and even primarily a school for nurses, based on the model designed by Florence Nightingale in England. The teaching was mainly practical in nature, but there was a philosophy behind it. Hélène applied, was admitted, spent two years in Bordeaux, and then as many again in Lorient, where there was a second Nightingale centre, obtained her diploma as a nurse and practiced this profession for a few years after that. She spoke readily of these years at the hospital, recounting with some amusement the dreadful situations she frequently found herself in, notably in the wards where they treated rabies. The livid greys and blacks of the 'sad hospital' in Baudelaire's 'Les Phares' (The Beacons), the screams and hallucinations in Goya's *Yard with Lunatics*, were still very much present in those places. It was a hard life for a young girl, the hours long and the situation sometimes dangerous, since people with rabies have an urge to bite. But her temperament, which turned out to be intrepid, made her remember it all fondly, for it was there she recovered her pride.

Yes, she had disappointed her father, and alarmed her parents in choosing a calling that was not, to use a word from that period, really 'suitable'; but she had done so in order to provoke, which revealed her attachment, and she could therefore return to Ambeyrac regularly, without having to justify herself too much, except for the feeling she was no longer quite worthy of her book-loving father which had not left her. And it goes to explain her behaviour later on. She retained an immense nostalgia for her native village, for her childhood years there and for her father's regard for writing in relation to life. This was her own 'country', as she called it, in contrast to the successive lodgings of her adult life. Whenever she thought of it, her good humour, that was really a mask, would freeze and her gaze appeared to wander. On her last brief visit, which was to be the last of her life, I am told that she'd trembled from head to foot.

Viazac

I

My father was Marius Elie Bonnefoy, though everyone called him Elie, perhaps because he insisted on it as a child. His own country was not the one I have just described, even though it was very close, and his culture was also markedly different, despite much that was obviously common to both. The part of the Lot Valley with its fine houses, often enough, primarily on the southern Aveyron side, with the towns of Villefranche-de-Rouergue and Rodez behind, must have seemed to him, I would venture, something like the Roman province in the eyes of the Celt further to the North. He was actually born no further than twenty or thirty kilometres from Ambeyrac, scarcely more: but getting there by way of little roads and rivers to cross—the Célé flowed nearby, a little tributary of the Lot—was enough to give an impression of distance, all the more so because the country he hailed from was as I have said, much tougher, and the high plateau just close by, sparsely populated, with its shepherd tracks, stones, bushes and animals darting furtively across. People had different aspirations in these isolated regions, and different bearings. On one side, to the North, were the semi-deserted areas around Rocamadour, the religious centre, and to the North-East, ten kilometres away, was the Cantal, starting with Maurs.

In those days, people scarcely ever left the village. As a child my father knew only the closest to his own, Viazac: Felzins, Cardaillac, site of some obscure apparitions, and Figeac on market day. His first journey, not a long one, had been to Rocamadour because the priests had come to Viazac on a recruitment drive. They went from door to door: 'Have you a little boy, that we can make into a good priest? We will take him to the little seminary and look after his studies.' My grandfather, Jean Bonnefoy, a modest innkeeper, part-time tailor and barber to a few dozen peasants, let them take the little Elie, who spent two years at Rocamadour tracing, between two catechism classes, circles and ovoids, straight lines and right angles on his copybooks. And then one night, disliking the life there, he jumped with his bag out of the dormitory window and returned on foot to Viazac.

'So you don't want to be a priest', said his father, 'very well then, but you'll have to fend for yourself.' And a few weeks later he left once more, this time in a cart perhaps, in the other direction to Maurs where a cousin, a blacksmith, took him on as an apprentice. Maurs belonged essentially to the same world as Viazac, which was nearly within walking distance, and Elie scarcely had a chance to discover the society of his time before he was once again, without transition, confined, this time as a conscript doing military service, apprenticed to prepare the next war of revenge. It was easy to turn these peasants, resigned from birth, into cannon fodder for the great clash of arms.

And moulded in this way, Elie would have had little hope of surviving the war that broke out soon after, but life decided otherwise. At Maurs he had become a blacksmith and a boiler maker, and when his military service ended, in 1911, he got a job on the railways in Clermont-Ferrand, then in Montluçon and finally in the great workshops of Tours. Beating metal into shape for locomotives became, in 1914 at the time of the mobilization, such essential work for the new requirements, that the army engaged him to keep working where he was. Night and day, throughout the war, he made locomotives, and also the 75 cannon. His entire life was spent to-ing and fro-ing from the workshop to his lodgings, sometimes in the middle of the night. And no leave away whatsoever, except for short visits to his parents; and no friendships apart from his comrades at work, not even, so far as I know, any friends from childhood or adolescence, that later on have such different destinies in different places. There was little contact with the neighbours in Tours either, for whom my father was pretty much a foreigner, nothing at all apart from the occasional meeting with a certain Monsieur Peygourié and his wife and daughter, who hailed from the 'old country', whom we met on Sunday afternoon three or four times a year, without finding much to say to them.

I nearly forgot the ritual visits to the owner of the house, M. Gallé, on New Year's Day or at Epiphany. We were welcomed, a flight or two up the stairs, by a glass of white wine and a *galette* whose layered pastry I detested, and with it the fear of getting the Epiphany 'bean', which brought with it the embarrassment of having to wear the crown.[5] Even on these occasions, when good spirits and laughter were expected, my father remained silent. Just as on the walk through the streets, or in the garden, his gaze seemed distracted, seeking something elsewhere.

His destiny, an empty envelope. His life, a blank page. Even more so because Elie had scarcely read any books. This was less by lack of interest or opportunity—my mother read novels, we had a small library at home, which was soon enriched by the books inherited from her father—than by the fact that he didn't really know what it meant to read. From early childhood he held in his hands, that were soon roughened, nothing but tools and basic manuals. Apart from the newspaper, that he read through conscientiously each day, the only contact he had with printed matter beyond the immediately practical consisted of two or three folded pages—a song, with music and words, and with a drawing on the title page—that people at that time could buy at the market. But he did have one book, a big volume bound in red of which he was proud, on the history of locomotives; but he did not read it, he contented himself with looking at

5 At the feast of Epiphany, ('le jour des Rois') the visit of the Magi to the infant Jesus is celebrated by the Church. On 6 January, the *fête de la galette* is celebrated by French families, whether religious or secular. A tart made of layered marzipan pastry is consumed, in which a *fève* or bean is concealed. The person who gets the bean in his or her slice must then wear a golden cardboard crown, sold along with the tart at the baker's.

it, and it was his way of presenting to others, in fact to his children and his wife, the machines he made, that were his pride and joy. Machines he should like to have driven himself, I believe. alone in the streaming, sooty smoke, with the rails passing endlessly under the wheels. No books, nothing to nourish the imagination or the memory, and it was never going to be my father, be it said in passing, who could have read a bedtime story or told a tall tale out of his own life to a child.

He regretted this, undoubtedly, and it remained for him a thwarted, repressed desire. On Sundays, when he put his best suit on, he took care to let the morning newspaper peek out of one of his pockets. He would also bring back from the workshop big notebooks, broader than they were tall, with yellow paper, old registers with pages you could write or draw on the back of, which he knew I loved to do. It was as if, through these objects that came from the place where life had confined him, he were communicating something to me: that I should change their nature by means of the words I would write in them, and show that the workshop was not his only horizon. And yet I made no use of these notebooks, put off by their rubrics and columns. Which left me feeling somewhat guilty, and I rather think that my lifelong habit of writing on the back of used or printed sheets of paper may originate from this experience. I shall perhaps come back to this point.

II

But first I need to solicit further memories, and I shall evoke the relationship between Elie and Hélène, insofar as it appeared to me, early on. The differences between my parents were indeed great, but long too were the separations between the dawn and night on most days. Further, the work that each of them did was unintelligible to the other, unimaginable, even: all that Hélène received from Elie's days at the factory were his 'bleus', the blue work overalls that came back soiled, streaked with oily grease, to be plunged without delay into the washing machine that encumbered the kitchen. And yet I believe that real feeling had united them, from the first day, and nothing could ever break that link.

They had not met before committing to one another. Their union had been postulated by one of those matchmakers that existed in the villages at that time, whose vocation was to ensure—by means of their intimate knowledge of families and their pasts, their property, revenue, possible family ties—a degree of exogamy in that closed world. Showing admirable width of reference, for Ambeyrac and Viazac did not belong to the same world, this woman whom I imagine to be old, fragile, sitting for whole afternoons behind the curtains of her little window, had made a link between the two families, who did not know each other at all; and both families declared an interest. On one side, a boy just returned from military service, in good health and with a good job. On the other, a girl slightly his superior socially, but whose job as a nurse had rather relegated her in terms of class. Both sides were respectable, free of debt, committed to decency and hard work. It remained that the two young people should be suited to one another, as arranged marriages were something of the past.

I imagine that Hélène agreed to go along with the meeting, partly out of a wish to please her father, before whom she still felt guilty, but also out of pride. Let her teacher sister Lucie marry a teacher! She did not seek to contest the assumption behind the offer that was being made to her: that it was quite natural for her to marry a boilermaker, and thus she should be quite content with the match.

I am trying to imagine the meeting between the two families, each one presenting their offspring. It took place in Viazac, one Sunday. Having come by foot from Ambeyrac, the Maury family had taken the morning train from Toirac to Capdenac, two stations further on, and then a bus for about the same distance. At Viazac, they had emerged from the station at around lunchtime, almost opposite the house where they were expected, for the Hôtel Bonnefoy was also the Hôtel de la Gare, very nearly the only house anywhere in sight.

A moment taken, to size each other up. Two fathers and two mothers, sharing common rules of good conduct, but with two different ways of appraising and weighing each other up. The suitor's father, the innkeeper, cut the hair of peasants in the neighbourhood, and cut their clothes as well, especially their work overalls—and his speech, mannerisms and dress were consistent with that. The visitors were better dressed, with ties and, for the women, a brooch on the blouse, but they knew that the cooking was good in Viazac, and knew that the same could not be said of home. Christine *née* Artigues, my future paternal grandmother, who fed the young men who stopped for the night at the inn, travelling salesmen for the most part, was a virtuoso of rich cooking, famed throughout the region. Marie Chabert, Mme Maury, who was prudent, and also poorer than people imagined—her father had taken on the debts of a distant relation—would go to the carpenter in Ambeyrac and get handfuls of fresh sawdust, that she would pack into big round corrugated tins, old coffee tins; then, by means of two holes that she made in the base, for the air, she would turn them into a slow-burning fire that produced a smell of hot wood that—having smelled it—I knew to be intoxicating, in the gloom of the kitchen, though not really suitable for major culinary projects.

And suddenly, in the middle of this sumptuous meal, with its numerous courses, its tentative and doubtless rather awkward conversation, the young man being presented to the young woman declared that the food didn't suit him at all, but no matter, he would go and cook some eggs, at which he was apparently an adept. Exclamations, slightly embarrassed laughter. His action might have seemed coarse. And made his generally taciturn, possibly hostile behaviour during the meal more pronounced. My mother used to recount this scene, with an amusement that kept alive the keen sympathy she felt at the time, and that I understand. The impulsive declaration was not an expression of hostility towards the cook, but was designed to startle the girl at the other end of the table, thereby signalling his interest, and even an offer of marriage.

We don't need all this, he was saying, together we can start another sort of life, which I have the means to support. All this? He didn't mean the company and their manners, that my parents never ever criticized, but rather the past they perpetuated, the whole way of ordering things that resulted in the kind of meeting arranged that day. Elie was offering Hélène a new life, and too bad if, whether to start with or always, poverty would be part of it, as symbolized by the eggs. His action looked like a 'declaration', as people used to say. Very like an offer.

And Hélène had accepted the offer. Everything persuades me into thinking that the reasoned arrangement between the families led to an affectionate and even loving relationship, and that the first years my parents spent together were happy ones, despite the poverty and the hardships and exhaustion caused by the war. Of those first years, and even at times of the later ones, I have memories that I have already described in *Two Stages* and *Les planches courbes* (The Curved Planks) that strengthen this conviction. Sometimes my mother got angry, and even flew into rages, with anger in her voice, that terrified me, since I could not understand the reason for them. But even if, to this day, I do not know why, I do not think they were directed at my father. And I was struck, and comforted, by their obvious moments of closeness.

These latter were all too seldom, alas, the days being so busy and full of troubles, the needs of the growing family soon exceeding income. And they did nothing to lessen the anxiety that my father's silence caused me, that I felt as soon as I was of an age to observe and sense difficulty.

What I feared, especially so when I became aware of his failing health, was that he felt unworthy, as life passed and changed, of the alliance he had proposed to Hélène all those years ago, that she had accepted and that even now she never went back upon.

III

His companion no longer worked as a nurse, in fact, or was busy with tasks that did not oblige the factory worker that he remained to fret about his own standing. For a reason I'd never understood, Hélène had given up her profession, and had become instead a supply teacher, and though the task was a humble and precarious one, obliging her to run from one end of town to the other, in replacement postings that lasted only a few days—she did not possess the diplomas that could have advanced her—it meant that she now fraternized, during the recreation time, with qualified teachers who had knowledge, and even literary interests. It also meant that she had to work up her geography and history, and her arithmetic, and the poetry and fiction that she had never had the leisure to do before. Basic study manuals made their appearance at home, and the relationship with her sister Lucie, who would end her career in the Aveyron in the highest possible position for a teacher, as the headmistress of a school—the same school incidentally where her father had studied—was re-established, affinities and links renewed, that made of Hélène once again the daughter of Auguste Maury.

What is more, on his retirement, Auguste quit the little flat that went with his post at the school in Ambeyrac—a few small rooms in the town hall—for a lovely house on the other side of the Lot: a quite unexpected location that had big rooms and fine trees on terraces, where every summer he could receive his daughters and their children. The move from Ambeyrac to Toirac, which was really just over the bridge, barely an hour's walk, was nevertheless a major event in the lives of my grandparents. They had furnished it them-selves, Auguste Maury had space to shelve his books, and he even took with him the 'school museum' that he had put together over time—an ostrich egg, an iguana in a bowl and some other curiosities used to amaze his pupils—and a life for a long time confined opened up to the world and also to the century of the immediate post-war.

These changes were not, however, favourable to Elie, who must have felt in this new place even more of an out-sider. The school holidays were much longer than his. He would accompany us on the journey south, on the night trains, and these were precious times spent together, but soon he would have to leave again; even at Toirac itself, where Lucie's two sons and her daughter were all laughter and animation—humming the latest tunes, and sunbathing, which was another novelty of the time—he felt other, and kept himself apart. So much so, in fact, that it was at Toirac I really started to worry about him, especially since I too was pretty much left on my own. My sister and her cousins were all about ten years or so older than I, and their interests, desires, occupations meant nothing at all to me, who scarcely existed in their eyes. But in my solitude I was not in the least unhappy. I loved the house, the place, the countryside, and I felt that they were nourishing me at the deepest level, that they conferred on me a future, and a force. Whereas my father's isolation was quite clearly sterile.

The years that followed, after 1930, made matters worse. Nothing much changed during the summer months, but my grandfather died, then his wife—she lasted many long days, accompanied by Hélène, and I with her, wandering through the house filled with the groans of the dying woman, or braving the tracks on the ridgeway—and then the little inheritance my parents received set them looking for a larger place to live, a desire shared by the children who had grown. The small sum of money was used to rent and do up the maisonette I have already mentioned: expensive paintwork, furniture purchased from the big store that had just opened, another post-war novelty, and the whole thing solemnized by a huge radio set in the form of a cathedral. But this 'progress' was an illusion.

I have already mentioned this a little. My father lost the little garden that had occupied him earlier. He set up a kind of workshop in the small shed in the yard, with a work table and a little anvil, but what was the purpose of finding on a Sunday, without much use for them, the same tools as throughout the week? As exhaustion, and then illness overtook him, he scarcely ever went in there, especially as he used up so much energy walking to and from his work, four times a day. His diabetes, meanwhile, which had started before the move, weakened him further. I can still see, on the rue Galpin-Thiou, our first house, the supper table pushed back to make way for the bed to which Hélène would bring the little round tins that contained the dying leeches, destined for the cups that she would apply to Elie's back: wet cups, as they were then called, red and raw, on which those black worms sated themselves blindly.

On the rue Lobin, I no longer saw all this, since my parents now had a room of their own, but I knew with certainty that these leeches were of no use, and nor were the pancakes, made of black wheat with water and no salt, that made up the strict diet prescribed by the doctor. No, the new house did not represent the new start so naively hoped for. In vain did my mother try to boast of her pancakes that she stacked in tall piles every day, claiming that this was good, tough Auvergnat or Breton food, eaten by tough people, who were obviously superior to the salad and vegetable eaters of the Val de Loire; I could see her face grow increasingly lined with worry.

The last years were unhappy. The blue work overalls had become very incongruous items in the new environment. My father had grown fat, which humiliated him, as it smacked of poverty. Did the offer he had made Hélène all those years ago still have any meaning? Had it ever had? Was the wife's affection not merely a form of courageous resignation? These are probably the questions Elie asked himself at the end of his life.

Then came May 1936. Some days previously, he had been diagnosed with phlebitis. My father was in bed, with instructions not to get up abruptly. There were several sprigs of lily-of-the-valley in the room, since it was the season, which the neighbours had given to Hélène, whose birthday it was that day. She was now forty-seven years old. I meanwhile was meandering home slowly from the Lycée; it was early afternoon, and I was lingering in the streets with one or two classmates. I saw my mother on the doorstep, I was brought up short, and then I ran. Yes, it was indeed me she was waiting for, and on the instant: 'You must come and see,' she said, and seizing my hand she led me up the stairs to their room.

IV

I am perfectly familiar with what the psychoanalysts have to say about the Oedipus complex, that rivalry between father and son, those sudden accesses of murderous hatred towards each other, and the effects of this ambivalent relation throughout the conscious and unconscious life of the child who remains a prisoner of it, that leads sometimes to lasting estrangement, or worse still to a feeling of guilt, more or less intense. And I am quite willing to believe that these facts are real, and sadly that they did drive some of the thoughts I entertained before this premature death, and that they did not dissipate at the dreadful vision of it, in the hollow of a disordered bed.

And yet I cannot stop myself from believing that a quite different feeling can invade, at least sometimes, the child observant of his father and his mother, and that is because the other forces act upon him do not originate in the body, in its instincts and drives, but in a conflict intrinsic to the use of words, born of a difficulty that affects language at its deepest level. I have already developed this idea on a few occasions, possibly because the memories I have just evoked and the anxiety they give rise to in me obliges me to do so; here I shall just give a summary, as I think it explains much about the relationship with my father.

In what does this consist? In an event that takes place at the heart of speech, whose consequences leave a trace at all levels and at every instant of life. Words are by their nature denotative, they can summon up in the mind a memory of something in its immediacy, and by the same token in its unity, its fullness of presence, undivided. But to think and to act, one must be able to perceive in this primary presence aspects one can lean upon in order to compare them with others existing in other things. To do this is to substitute for certain aspects, a montage, partial and abstract representations, whereby a removal is enacted from what is at play when the object is still whole: that is an existence, in its place, in its moment, in its infiniteness, in its finitude. The self continues to exist, in the scheme of time that ends with death. But everywhere and all around there is now only matter, consisting of objects one wants to possess, to have and no longer to be. We are no longer of the world, as Rimbaud cried out. The word that uttered the plenitude of life has had to subordinate itself to the concept, which engenders only images.

And must this sudden, vast divide between what is and its representation—its image in thought—not be understood also as what, at the start of life, will trouble the relationship of the child with its parents? Spontaneously, for him, the word is one with what it shows, 'Look, this is your house, look, this is a flower', and he too is one with all these other lives; it is the golden age of the mind which the poets have sung, and with such nostalgia, Wordsworth in the 'Immortality Ode', Baudelaire in 'Moesta et errabunda', Rimbaud in 'Jeunesse'. The little child is one 'with the world' for a short season, and his mother is for him the great guide, who speaks his language, crystallizing his experience of what is a gathering of presences, into a place, which leads in later life to those dreams of a *hortus conclusus*. That there is anything outside of this world is still barely apprehended, in bad dreams.

But what then is the father, if not the being who returns in the evening from this outside, that is still unknown, and whose speech constitutes another way of saying, of living? The work he does obliges him to employ conceptual thought, he must speak its abstraction, and his words deprive him of the possibility of having with the nearby tree, the creaking gate along the path, the link of immediacy that is all at once to touch, to see, to breathe, to feel. And however great the affection the little child feels for him, will the father not come to be the intruder who will put an end to the child's present state of being in the world? The father comes to represent analytical knowledge, that knows nothing of specific existences, and when the door opens and he comes in, he can cause fear, he can rouse hostility. He is the invader, who brings with him a glimpse of non-being into the space of being, and a shadow that falls even in the light of a summer's day.

To put this another way: the father is only one element of the Oedipus complex, he is also and perhaps above all the protagonist in a drama in which the future of language is at stake. And there is no doubt that within this other complex—let us call it the Orpheus complex—the father must play the detestable role of the god of the dead, the god who stole from the singer his earliest companion.

But is this enemy not seen sometimes, and principally, as a victim to be pitied? Very often the father comes home more crushed by the words of the outside than the fashioner of their hard necessity. Sometimes even he speaks them less, choosing rather than to teach them, to keep silent, noting in his son or daughter, with obvious sadness, their way of existing he is excluded from by destiny. Conceptual thought has victims as well as triumphant zealots. A number of those who have to use it, do so with a regret that eats at them. And the child still young enough to understand what words can add to life, how could he rise up against his father when the latter is so clearly struggling with a discourse that stifles them? On the contrary, he will feel compassion for him, he will dream of delivering him from his servitude.

I can see myself on the threshold of the room my mother led me to on that May day, undoubtedly the last day of my childhood, and I am convinced that the kind of compassion I am describing was at the heart of my relation with Elie, my father. He hadn't been the tyrant, but the victim. He had never liked adult discourse—his silence was proof enough of that—and all he had done was lose the words of his early childhood, without being able to replace them with those that analyse and legislate: he never benefited from their promises, and their powers. I had no reason therefore to cast him as the ogre of dangerous thinking, I had rather to pity, and to suffer for him, with him.

V

I need to nuance my description of this compassion, which must not be understood as an experience of any great spiritual scope with which I might credit myself. True, there does exist a type of compassion that devotes itself body and soul to the sufferings of others, to bodily suffering and to mental suffering. This way of behaving, this relation to the self in the presence of the other, involves a forgetfulness of what one is, a sacrifice that is as spontaneous as it is lasting of desires one might experience, in fact they exist no longer in the mind or the flesh, every shred of egocentricity inherent in the life of the body having been swept away by an overwhelming emotion. And in return, in the gift one makes of oneself, the being can intervene, which is the transmutation of the nothingness of the world by the event of this gift offered and accepted. It is what Goya depicts when he paints his doctor leaning over him, when he came close to death. It is a self-portrait expressing gratitude to a particular person, but it also bears witness to his newfound faith in human relations, the dawning of a light where he supposed there was nothing but darkness.

Compassion can be the foundation, and the re-founding, of being. But it is certainly not this lofty feeling I had in regard to my father. What I am speaking of is something much more ordinary, and in no way fully divested of personal interest. Where did this emotion, this restlessness of mind come from? It is the concern one feels on grasping that someone is suffering as a result of being deprived of the words that would enable him to exist 'in the world'. That a regret subsists in him which stops him finding value in the discourse taught him later, that he might have benefited from, or even enjoyed. And one suffers oneself, one suffers for him, but—and that 'but' is crucial—without losing sight of who one is oneself, with one's ambitions and desires: to the point of thinking—or at least hoping—that what one wants to be some day might remedy, if only in a small way, the suffering of which one has taken cognizance.

I need to dwell a little, in passing, on the nature and the narrowly delimited compassion that I call poetic. It represents hope for the other human being who suffers from aphasia. But it also entails a fear for the self, since it cannot but fear that he who feels it won't end up falling into the same negative silence that he currently deplores. It means also that the compassionate one conducts an examination of his own thought, which is difficult to do, even painful. But it will remain a relation to the self, an exercise of the self, resulting in the kind of happiness that can come from this kind of introspection. This relation to the self? To reach in one's own words the ridge where they are out in the light, one must frequent as far as possible the shadowy regions, where these most ordinary desires are produced.

Personal desire remains within poetic compassion as central and active as anxiety about another person. Little will have been sacrificed of the potential one feels that one bears, and there may even be benefits to be gained from the feeling that one is able to preserve that vision of the world that refreshes it, and which, now de-familiarized can renew societies. And yet, the picture I need to draw need not be so dark. Life and the promise of life remains in the élan that opens us to others. And the alliance we propose to have with them is the one valid thing, the only valid thing if we are to have a future. To suffer from their silence, is in fact to wait upon them until they try to emerge from it, it represents an offer to begin working together with them in the substrata of language.

VI

Does what I have just said—what I have just said to myself—make any sense? Is it not merely a dream of the intellect, born out of the concern I had for my father whose unhappiness I could see? It is true that these ideas are only too consonant with several aspects of my childhood. Still, I have no doubt that they are founded.

I believe this even more so in that they clarify for me, today, moments I had lived through without really under-standing, but with so much emotion that I still remember them. For example, it was exactly this mixture of compassion and the need to appease my own anxiety that possessed me one morning around 1930, when my father, the working man with short holidays, went to Toirac to take the train home, after a stay with us that was all too brief. It was high summer, the weather fine. The whole family had accompanied Elie to the station, and everyone around him was chattering, as they waited for the local train. Meanwhile, child that I still was, I conceived the idea of giving him a good-luck charm, and wandered off as far as the switch, where the platform was overgrown with grass, already a part of the surrounding countryside. At this point, the track was covered for a few metres with clover, densely packed, dark little leaves spread across the ground, and my dearest wish was to find one with four leaves, that kind that brings happiness and prosperity.

So I started looking, bent over, and went down on my knees. But there was nothing other than the ordinary variety, and time was ticking away, the train was getting nearer, I could already hear it echoing through the valley, so what could I do, other than pick a three-leaf clover, and by means of my saliva, try and stick to it a fourth leaf. Such a delicate task, alas, I was all fingers and thumbs, clumsy and impatient, and with the train about to come to a halt, steaming noisily. And I felt a real stab of sorrow then, which has remained in my memory, sorrow for the man over there, on the platform, to whom I had to run before he left. But so many ambiguities had clustered around this plan of mine, in its ambition, and in its failure, that I've begun to understand only now! The clover that I'd wanted to give him, was also I now see—nature modified, and redeemed, with that extra leaf, a miracle worked by my own saliva, my voice—an emblem, still obscure, of what I wanted for myself, to work as close to language as possible and possibly in relation to other beings, but also as an individual project, which involved the risk that the initial altruistic *élan* would collapse on itself, become artificial and come undone, and that the leaf added to the other three would be thus unable to unite by an act of the mind what nature had proposed otherwise.

Toulouse

I

This is the point at which I once again take up Toulouse, and its meaning, that was hidden from me.

Toulouse, because no sooner had I understood that my father was present in *The Red Scarf* than I understood also why I had situated the unimagined and quite possibly unimaginable suite of the poem in that city. It was this enigma—one of those that seemed designed to encourage me to forget about these pages—that prompted me now to inquire, something that I had more or less avoided up till then, into the nature of the link that united, or perhaps otherwise, my father and my mother, Elie, Hélène.

But the reason Toulouse was at work in my unconscious as the figure and link between these lives, I was to discover all of a sudden, and I shall now attempt to explain it, but I must first return to what I have said about my parents' origins.

I said that my father, from Viazac, a stone's throw from the Cantal, considered himself an authentic Auvergnat, a conviction charged with meaning at a deep level in his consciousness. For those who claimed to come from there, the Auvergne at this time was very much a *place*, in the strong sense of that word. With its extinct volcanoes and its pastures, and elsewhere its forests of chestnut and its moors, with its population reputed as rebellious since the Gallic Wars, and unassimilated by other cultures, the Auvergne figures in the mind as somewhere autonomous and apart, enjoying a natural prestige, which was proudly experienced as such by its inhabitants. It *was*, it had its being, and in more abundance than what the trains that moved slowly in, stopping at stations with strange names, might already suggest. It seemed to escape speech, and even language, to appear as something almost transcendent, an *arrière-pays* on the edges of the nation. In short, it was silence, when all about it existed ordinary parlance. It was a way of staying within one's thoughts, in the mind, and in its dreams, which goes some way to explaining the silence of my father, who felt so strongly that he came from 'down there'.

On my mother's 'side' there was, by contrast, language. The Auvergne certainly held some sway over the Aveyron, and the *bougnats*, the Auvergnats who went to Paris and sold wine and coal, and who owned restaurants, were frequently if not preeminently from the Aveyron, but they came from the deep countryside, from those moorlands that prolong the Cantal and the Lot, whereas another culture was dominant at Villefranche-de-Rouergue and at Rodez, and one which was consonant, this time, with a number of intelligible significations, that were explicit, shareable and rooted in historical tradition.

The high spiritual civilization that flowered under the counts of Toulouse, and that had at all times remained open to other parts of the world, with their traditions, thought and very diverse religious practices that were at times antagonistic, still survived vestigially in those towns. The Roman Empire declined and came apart, but its language survived, transformed simply, the intuitions of its Latin past remained alive, and secretly fed the new languages. This part of Southern France, bordering on the Pyrenees, with its rich and fecund lands, was one of the high points of the Latin inheritance. Poetry itself re-emerged in Occitan, with the Troubadours, whose visions were erotic as much as religious.

All this made a world, and the city that contained it and drew such prestige from it, was a metaphysical resource for my maternal ancestors, just as the Auvergne was for my father. At the centre of all the frenetic activity carrying on between the Rhône and the Atlantic littoral stood Toulouse, incontestably its capital, with a vigour and a panache that remained alive, even in my grandfather's time, who was certainly conscious of it, and even I dare say, very attached to it. Did he consider himself an Auvergnat? He was primarily the village school teacher, concerned with the transmission of culture, and he could not therefore have been insensible to the past and present of the metropolis whose patois, into which he had been born turned out to be an entire and autonomous language, with its own literature that still flourishes today. What is more, his family name was Maury, a name that was borne by some dignitaries in Toulouse, as he liked to remind people; and he had married, possibly with this thought in mind, a girl whose ancestry was Toulousain.

During that meeting at Viazac in 1912 between the families of Elie and Hélène, it might be that Toulouse could represent what marked out their differences. Even if I am inclined to think that, as soon as they broke into patois at that festive table—as they were sure to have done, at the sight of the dishes served—subtle nuances would have transpired, not so much in the words themselves as in the way they were spoken. On one side, there would have been the language of the Bonnefoys, held in check by the silence of the Auvergne, lived instinctively, made of less syntax and more allusion; and on the other were more complex turns of speech, more conscious of their allure, such as you might find in books. Who knows, it is perhaps when he realized these differences, that marked him out as a peasant, that Elie in some humiliation quit the table for that moment. The eggs that he cooked, alone in the gloomy kitchen, did not equal the more elaborate dishes they were discussing in the next room, with recipes being divulged, even that requiring usage of secondary aspects of the language, rather than its fundamentals. The eggs represented less of a temptation to nuance the language and to embellish it uselessly. And the way in which he presented the idea of them, almost brusquely, was really a declaration to the woman with whom he would have to share everything, that asserted the primacy of a place where simple objects spoke out their presence in a way that predated all languages. The region of the Auvergne was asserted, and was magnified, confronted with civilization as represented by Toulouse.

II

On one side, then, is the obscure conviction that reality is more than words; and on the other, a certain ease with them, and an interest in the things that are born from them.

And lodged within this opposition is something that enables me to elucidate one of the enigmas of my 'Red Scarf': why was it that the man who formerly lived in the house with white walls and with its deep recesses—a real house, like the one handed down in families—why was it that he lived in Toulouse, lodging in a hotel? And above all, why was it in this hotel at Toulouse that he had spent so many years of his life, and why were they spent like the final days of his existence? Alas, the thing had become sadly obvious. Why Toulouse? Because my father was obliged, through marriage—whereby a peasant entered a family of teachers—to spend his life in the unfamiliar world represented for him by Toulouse. And why at a hotel? Because in this other place, this other milieu, he had never felt completely at home; because he felt like a foreigner who can never quite call the place home. And why should his wife, who was from Toulouse, have to share this room with him, if not by chance obviously, and why would she accept the discomfort in doing this to the point of sacrificing her own life choices? Because she loved him, because she had sacrificed for him the happier and more meaningful existence she could have had in her own world, so visibly did her attachment and her nostalgia for it remain.

The hotel room in Toulouse is the allegory of the life and destiny of my father, and of his own anxiety. And it represents the confirmation of what I feared for him, well before I received that letter in my poem. I saw, and very early on, that my father was living in what was for me a natural place to exist, but that for him was a place where he did not feel entirely at home. Like someone so absorbed by his predicament, his guilt, his sadness, that he was, deep in himself, the man *The Red Scarf* had revealed to me: an exile cut off from his origins, a man alone with his captive companion, a sad soul who, in this hotel room, had lived without children.

Without children? Had I not then existed in my father's eyes? Of course I had! But I fear, not in a way that could have lessened his unease. He expected a lot from me, certainly, right up to the end. But he saw in me also the stranger that my narrative confronted him with—in the room where 'everything was grey', because 'night was falling'—and who had with him, so it seemed to him in the gloom, an astonishing and mysterious red scarf. A stranger come from Paris, what is more: the city for my father of unfathomable lives and unimaginable choices. In *The Red Scarf*, the man who came from Toulouse is my father, and the man he meets at nightfall is me, disguised as a stranger with whom he leaves, on the off chance, his address. But fearing at the same time, that he would wait in vain for a letter.

III

And here I am compelled to the second remark that flows from the perceived meaning of the red scarf: that red, the colour of blood, which striped our chests around the dark heart. 'This man, elderly now', who pores over his past, is me, again, but not at all as what remains of one in a fiction built out of a dream: no, fully even if bent over and closed in on himself, that man is the man I am, with all his desires, whether he knows them or not, all his ambitions, memories, lacunae, his entire life in fact, and possibly with all his potential still, or in any case that part of it still accessible to someone who has grown old.

The personage who has emerged under my pen is me, with all I have repressed, all the feelings and presentiments left untended: how can this be doubted when I find, in this impulsive text, Danäe, the two swords, 'the hyacinth girl', which are all facts in my real life even if in an excess of self-consciousness at the moment of their emergence? Instants of profound surprise, shocks whose emotion I had not properly gauged, nor what they signalled, which I consigned to my notebooks so I could reflect on them one day, I did not know when.

It was me, the actual being—not the implied self of the work, the aesthetic self—who wrote these lines, and accompanying this, tangential to this was a duty to locate myself, and to understand, what I had not attended to when I noted down the fragment of this text, and that I had been tempted to suppress because I could not bring it to a conclusion. It was, moreover, a repression that pitched me into the one which had ensnared me earlier. For those years, of the two swords, of reading Malory and T. S. Eliot, of Danäe— Rembrandt's Danäe—were when I imagined my only task was to reflect upon the essence and the future of poetry, matters which distracted me from more personal problems, even if they were in fact a consequence of them, if not indeed a displacement. Ah, that time must come to an end! I must know myself better, and better reveal why I should desire that, and why I have so often undertaken it; even my first published piece of writing—in reply to a survey, brazenly and provocatively seeking views on 'Le savoir-vivre'—responded in the same vein. But in fact I escaped myself in words quite as much as I sought myself: and now it is time, high time, to ask myself real questions.

That piercing red—for a speech so clearly impossible in all that black-and-white narration—is it not in fact the most striking fashion for this need to make itself felt? I have said that the red scarf is an emblem of the blood-tie, of red blood. And the fabric that two men have seen laid over each other's hearts—this is a father before his son. But this red, whether dreamt or transcendental, is also, is it not, the fruit of the mind—with its intuitions— stamping itself above ordinary thought. And it leads us to reflect on what there is in the direct bloodline, and in the exchange between father and son, that goes beyond the straightforward Oedipal drives and works to transgress what is in the natural order so as to render it more properly human. 'Love must be reinvented' wrote Rimbaud. One hesitates to use such a grand phrase, but what is at stake is precisely that.

A plan starts to take shape. *The Red Scarf* was not simply of the imagination, but it was preliminary to the return of memories and of unrecognized aspirations, and with it the acknowledgement of an obstacle, and possibly of a taboo, that stopped any forward development. And insofar as I continue to ponder this poem, as clearly I see that I have to, it must no longer be a question of providing a fiction with its missing ending but of trying to do what its mysterious interruption in fact required of me: to quit the plane of reverie, which avoids real problems—except at moments when they are glimpsed and therefore interrupted before they must be owned up to—and focus on my own life. And I must do this by analysing the 'Red Scarf' in all its textual detail, through the layers of signifiers that conceal meaning, but which can also reveal it, if one questions them patiently.

IV

Yes, I owe it to myself to ask the real questions, but now the memories come flooding back, as if my life could no longer wait for me to open some of its coffers, recognizing that the time has now come. What, for example, of the rooms painted in lime-wash, and of the sense of 'deliverance' that startling whiteness offered the one who remembers? Nothing could have plunged deeper and more directly into my existence before that 'twenty-fifth year', with all its needs that Surrealism, which I had for a period espoused, could not supply. From the first months of my life, when I had crawled along the walls finding bits that were unstuck and that I could tear off, right up until the five years I spent in a hotel room—did that already prefigure the metaphor of Toulouse?—I had almost always lived in rooms with flowery wallpaper. My desire for real flowers was frustrated by these dead stereotypes. I longed for something more breathable, and I recall my happiness when in 1946 I stayed for a few days with a young painter who I had been corresponding with, and I saw, all around me, white walls. It was in Cordes, in the Tarn, in an old house with deeply recessed windows; and it must have brought to mind the lost house in Toirac, whose stairwell was the same white, even though it was drowned in shadow. Cordes was a true discovery for me, in harmony with my real needs, and it is thus natural that it should have reappeared in *The Red Scarf*, that anamnesis.

And it was only very natural that my memory at work in this poem should make of a place where I had only stayed a few days—and which had quenched my long-standing thirst—the scene wherein I could realize, if still unconsciously, my desire! Cordes is close by Toulouse, one can come out from the city for a short visit, and my father in his Toulouse hotel could well have come out for an afternoon or an evening, to sit against the light of some big window and play out the fantasy I had of my relationship with him.

And what of the girl at the end of the first fragment of the poem, who comes in to the room 'where soon it will be dark', with a scarf in her hands? Ah, now I understand why the narrative had to stop! For the girl is none other than my mother, obviously, it is Hélène imagined at the moment in her life when she was to unite her destiny to my father's.

She enters the room with a scarf in her hands that has to be red, which can only be a gift that she has to offer. Was it that 'Sonnet pour Hélène', 'the evening Love brought you down to the room', my familiar, my perfect stranger?[6] And for you, was it not that moment, in doubt and in unknowing, when you made a decision whose consequences would be so grave that your chest tightens and your hands tremble? You are at home with your parents and your suitor has just arrived. Perhaps you are going to offer him that scarf whose folds store in sleep the blood of childbeds to come. Anguish, because the blood is your father's, to whom you are so attached precisely for what makes him different from other men, and probably from this one too.

V

I have fleshed out this instant because I understand its gravity, on every occasion. For anyone who is upstream of the kind of choice that changes a life, the things close at hand

6 Bonnefoy is quoting from the *Second Livre Sonnets des Amours pour Hélène* (1578) by Pierre de Ronsard, commissioned by Catherine de Médicis.

participate with him, or her, in the infinity of the possible, and they are coloured by it; it is to bathe once again in the light that early childhood laid over them. To make this kind of choice, is to commit to sharing with another for years to come, and to pledge oneself to a certain existence, to substitute the particular for the infinite, and for now these same things are still alive for an instant longer, but in peril of being reduced to what life's difficulties will make of them: the wherewithal one will or will not have, how to ease straitened circumstances, and furnish external material needs. The choice to be made puts being itself in danger. In order to ensure that tomorrow's realities will have the same plenitude as yesterday's, one needs to love them—to love them truly and deeply—for what they shall be, and how can one be sure to sustain that if in any way the alliance made today becomes even a little undone in the uncertain future? This is quite enough to worry the young woman who has come into the room, and it explains why, in *The Red Scarf*, the party arriving are seen in the *contre-jour* of a deeply recessed window.

Just these few words from *The Red Scarf*. The memory I described as 'fugitive', and now, so fertile!

VI

This entrance into the room, first of all, with the scarf in her hand, is the kind of vision one has in the first years of life: for the love a child feels for its mother in that hour of existence when things and people are to the same degree vivid presences in the primal light; the child's love is addressed to what in her partakes still, from the same live source of being in the world, and before the sacrifices that life imposes, it perceives her in her unfurling hope, when she imagines that her destiny is coming into flower. For the child, the mother remains perpetually that girl, despite and beyond the compassion he feels also for the woman he sees ageing, and worn down by material cares.

This in any case is what, for my part, I believe I felt. I find trace of it in those narratives that mix memory and dream; it explains my emotion when I read poems, or lines, like the passage in 'Ode to a Nightingale' where Keats writes of Ruth in exile, and just before a reunion in which her courage will be revealed: 'She stood in tears amid the alien corn'. The child feels for his mother a love that places her, virgin-like, metaphysically on a plane beyond limitations he feels that he will himself have to accept. And this is to dream of the transfiguration that must miraculously deliver her to her true self, but it is also to ask questions of oneself which are not anodyne. Will she have the strength of soul necessary to keep alive the hope, necessary for such an enterprise? And what about her companion, the husband, also growing old, and perhaps full of self-doubt—will he be any help to her in this ceaseless task?

VII

I write this, and then, returning to *The Red Scarf*, and thinking of the man in Toulouse who left his name on an envelope, I surmise that on the very day they met for the first time, he had quite possibly, feeling the same fear, asked himself the same question: already prey to the uneasiness that would darken his life. Entering the house at Ambeyrac, Elie must have wondered if he was worthy to receive the extraordinary gift of this scarf, signifying the red of being itself, and a chance to lift him out of the greyness of his daily existence. And as I write this, I am pierced by a thought that horrifies me.

I return to what my poem tells me about this first day. Now, I know my father is visiting the young woman's house, because the latter comes into the room as if she has come from her bedroom. And he wears the scarf over his breast, against his heart, which means that what Hélène was holding in her hands, it is he who has it now, she has made him the gift of it, which means that he is accepted, the alliance has been sealed. In my view, the opening lines of *The Red Scarf* state what has taken place. Not that this pseudo-memory of mine does not mean also that the lovely lightness of the white walls suggests my own devout wish that the gift was a true gift, and taken as such, so that in other words Elie would later have a reason to keep hope alive: at this first meeting, Hélène had loved him, she had put her trust in him, and they would remain bound together in a way their differences would certainly test but never endanger.

And obviously this is how I should want it to have been, that day, so that I should not be too alarmed by Elie's silence later on. On those late summer afternoons, from where I stood at the end of the garden, did I not sometimes see my parents sitting side by side at the window, partly open to benefit from the coolness afforded by a nearby tree? My father was home from work, and Hélène would speak to him, and he would reply, calmly, and a real exchange seemed to be taking place. And the evening light would sculpt their faces, it seemed both to unite and watch over them.

Yes, but the man in the red scarf, seated this time in the *contre-jour* at his other window, is also the man who will express himself, who will speak, in reply to the letter he certainly no longer expected. And what does he write? First, he is astonished not to have been forgotten. He too remembers, the house, and the person who has just sent him this letter. He knows also that there was a third person though he 'no longer dares' try to recall who she was. Who was she? The girl, obviously, who came into the room with the scarf still folded in her hands. But why does he dare not think of this? Could it be that the memory of her is too painful?

VIII

Alas, he says something else as well, and it's the end of his letter that scares me, just as it had already shocked the man 'elderly now', but it seems to me that was for another reason. My own fear does not spring from the thought of a breach in the laws of nature, or from the sound of a footfall in a house one knows to be empty, but it is still a shudder, a rush of anguish, a desire to hasten to Toulouse to repair something one fears irreparable.

And what does the man I have recognized as Elie, as my father, in fact say? That he remembers how the person who has just written to him would wear, as darkness fell, a 'large red scarf': and it was this that struck him, that returned in memory 'at moments of his life'.

A red scarf, which I must have worn, since I have identified myself as the protagonist of my narrative! Certainly, to reassure myself, I can try to make believe that the vision my father had was only his perception of the blood-tie between us, which the colour and the placing of the scarf turn into metaphor. But equally, I have to recall that the young woman had come into a place where, in the space of the dream, I too was present. Up until now I thought she had made the gift of the scarf to Elie, did he not wear it 'draped over his shoulders'? But what does he think? He thinks that the gift was made to me. And that is the obvious truth he has kept in his mind, which comes to torment him 'at moments of his life'.

And now I am left to imagine, ponder, revisit the past in a way that strikes me down with anguish. Did my father really believe that? Did he think that his wife had become more attached to her child than to him, recognizing in her son the blood that was her own, and leaving her husband, who was really no more than an intruder, in the half-light of that first evening? Oh, if that were indeed so, what sadness he must have felt! Frequently, as it was, he felt like a stranger at moments in his life, on the margins of Hélène's family. It was this feeling I thought that caused his silence, his withdrawal, of the distance, two steps behind, he would keep on Sunday walks; but I consoled myself by thinking that, at certain moments, the intimate bond they shared in the early days remained alive.

I thought that, and I think it still. But how much more difficult, and more tenuous, these comings together must have been if he reasoned that his wife's preference for me could only mean the rejection of a whole part of him! A further dimension to his solitude, and a reason to let himself go, into illness and death.

IX

I take the measure of this thought he may have had, and which now suddenly makes me fearful when I gauge the effect it had on his existence, and I am compelled to realize that— whether consciously or not, complicit or not—I must have been the cause of the unhappiness. Did my father really believe that the young woman he was ready to love was going to make a gift of the scarf to another, who was there, even if indistinct as yet, in the shadow: another who occupied the very heart of her own desire, her dearest wish? And was he correct in thinking this? On reflection, I have to say that, yes, alas, he was surely not mistaken in fearing that this preference, already latent within Hélène, would become manifest when the time came, and would leave him out on the doorstep of the house he could scarcely now call his own. And at this point also, I must reflect upon my role in the silence of his last years.

And was I in fact so unaware of the situation at the time, as my present astonishment might suggest? Again, I fear not, I think I always understood, if very confusedly, what was going on in this woman, who was at once cheerful and anxious, and courageous, clearly, and who instructed me in the rudiments of life. And I was aware of what went on in myself.

I need now to reread the various fragments of *The Red Scarf*, with this idea in mind. In the second version, which seems to be just a variant of the first, I stumble over a clue that troubles me. My stand-in in this text says that towards the man he remembers and who has not forgotten him he had nourished a 'feeling at once of hostility and fascination'.

Hostility! If the stranger in the poem does indeed represent my father, as I am persuaded, I must have experienced a kind of aversion for him, even if tempered by a large dose of ambivalence. And how am I to understand this feeling, which accords not at all with what I thought up until now when I reflected on, and spoke about Elie? Is this hostility just a late symptom, a vestige of the Oedipal confrontation? Or is it in fact a clue to the existence— and its survival—of a very different kind of confrontation; the one in which I had a role, that eventually cast a shadow over my parents' marriage? A role that was a lot less passive, and less unconscious, than I should like to think; for it involved adhering to Hélène's hopes for me, which in turn distanced me from my father.

Did I then see my father, at least on occasion, through the prism of an idea that she had of me, and which excluded him; and did that make him a stranger in my eyes too, an intruder? It is all too true that very early on in my childhood I came to love what I perceived thanks to the 'blue gaze' of my mother. I saw no lies, unlike Rimbaud recalling what he discovered at the same age—seven years old, the first experience of conceptual thought—in the eyes of Vitalie Cuif when they rested on him; I on the other hand felt an enrichment of reality. I became attached to what she always kept before her, the example of her own father, and this thought certainly preoccupied her and distracted her from current circumstances. I must therefore revise everything I have thought good to say so far. A dimension was lacking.

X

There exists a further clue, which compels me to think thus. It is in the fragment of the poem in which I tried to imagine what happened at Toulouse, when the son leaves the train and dashes to the hotel where the father is dying. 'He knocks on the door, she opens.' And there is a woman whose expression is 'distraught', I wrote, because she is living through a desperate moment. Her husband has disappeared, people are searching for him everywhere, 'he might be dead'. Now that

I know what the hotel at Toulouse stands for, I am in no doubt as to who 'this woman' is, even if those two almost hostile words try to mask that knowledge: obviously she is Hélène, and remembered as she was during those tragic minutes I have already recounted when, my father having only just died, she left his bedside for the street, where she waited for me to return from the Lycée. Her expression was certainly 'distraught' at that moment, strikingly so. And what is it she says to me, in the poem?

'You' she cries out, 'you!' There is no doubt that these words intend me to perceive—and to understand at last—a kind of expectation I had not suspected up until then, or that I had refused to see clearly. And I come to this realization at the moment the narrative breaks off with a suddenness that may well signify my desire to preserve at all costs my former misunderstanding. I observe also that in the intense animation the new arrival arouses there persists nevertheless a doubt as to who he is: because Hélène uses the formal *vous* form at that door in Toulouse, as if she were addressing a stranger, not her son. There is a passionate avowal, but also surprise, as at the end of a long wait. And on my part there is also an avowal, which follows immediately—that of my own knowledge— but it is followed instantly by a displacement, triggered by a fear whose meaning is not manifest. I wrote:

And he, arriving:
I recognize you, he says.
I know you,

but then straightaway:
A wall collapses
Between her and him.
Or else is it the bird of night
Who strikes their faces with its wings,

and with that, the regular flux of intuitions and memories that up to then constituted *The Red Scarf* ceased. I did not know or I did not wish to venture any further.

What does all this mean? That I had in fact always known what I represented for my mother in my early years, but I knew also that her preference was in part irrational, and there was a real danger that the desired alliance might fail. But I need also to explore further what lay behind the 'you, you!', the meaning of the collapsing wall and of the 'bird of night'. And of all the other mysteries, concealed beneath these! Where could the man be found, once his wife realized in panic that he had fled the hotel, even though he was ill, and gravely enough for her to fear he might be dead? As for the collapsing wall, I knew as soon as it occurred in this verse fragment, it was the pile of great stones, fallen in chaos in front of me, and that someone behind them was crying out, making signs that I had to decipher. And what of the black bird? What did it mean by beating its wings so violently, yet differently from Poe's great raven, since it was beating not against a door still closed but against human faces. There is certainly a long way to go, along a path I had thought, after all, forbidden me.

But just now I must revise and review another proof that I was not unaware of the special interest shown in me, and to which I responded with an emotion that answered my mother's own. This time the proof lies in a fact and not in a piece of writing. Even if the fact in question does involve a text, mention of which will come as no surprise to some of my readers. I mean my discovery in 1933—three years before my father's death, and just before I went to the Lycée—of the short novel *The Red Sands*.[7]

I have discussed all too fully, in a book[8] that I wrote seven years after *The Red Scarf*, my memory of this novel, which I in fact misremembered to a significant degree; but how can I not think of it now, at the point I have reached in these thoughts about my mother, before and after her marriage? An archaeologist in the Gobi desert, is seeking the ruins of a Roman city, but what transpires is that the city is still intact, and still inhabited, by men and women who speak in Latin. It had simply disappeared below the surface of the desert, an encroachment of more recent centuries, and settled at some oasis of the depths, with an underground stream, around which it had rebuilt its palaces and dwellings. And that idea in itself, I now realize, contained much to affect a

7 Léon Lambry, *Dans les sables rouge* (1933).

8 Here, Bonnefoy is referring to the volume *L'Arrière-pays*, available in English as *The Arrière-pays* (Stephen Romer trans.) (London: Seagull Books, 2012).

child who heard his parents speak patois—a patois derived from Latin—and who dreamed that this Occitan language, which was dying out, in fact expressed a way of being in the world mysteriously superior to that of the present day.

And who is it, searching for this Rome in the sands? A father accompanied by his son. The latter is an adolescent admired by his father, who wants to interest him in his own discipline, unceasingly presented as a scientific discipline ruled by reason, a level gaze that must exclude everything not strictly and materially proven. And when I reread these pages, this time, I thought of my father, not that he would have treated me to such a philosophy, but because I felt his great desire was to see me one day become an engineer, whose calculations would actually design the locomotives that he merely assembled, in the terrible heat of the workshop.

And no mother anywhere to be seen, what is more, no woman on the horizon, to worry about her two men, so far away, and for so long, in dangerous regions . . . The two archeologists meanwhile have reached the most desolate part of the desert, and it is here that they discover some vague ruins, and then find on waking, two days in a row, possibly placed over their very hearts, stone tablets telling them—in Latin—to advance no further.

There then begins the series of events that shook me to the core. The 'young boy', as he is called in the book, keeps guard throughout the next night to shed light on the mystery, and in the half-light of the moon he sees a girl, who brings the messages, disappear down a crack in the earth. He sets off in pursuit, down long underground corridors, badly lit by torches, and soon he is taken prisoner by the last of the Romans, of whom Cepheis is queen, even though she is only sixteen. It is decided that he shall be put to death, but the brave queen saves him, it's obvious that she has fallen in love with him as much as he has with her, as their conversations will show. But alas! Cepheis is under a prohibition, which she knows to be the barrier that their different worlds and civilizations would place between them. Most of all, she is afraid of her friend's father, who is advancing towards them, dynamiting rocks on the way. With the rest of her tribe, she flees towards places that are even more remote, under the desert.

She escapes, but before she does, she and I exchanged words, and they remained in my memory ever since. As for the boy, he returns to the underground city, since he cannot bear that Cepheis should have gone. And sure enough, he does find her, in the same palace-in-dream, where he spoke to her for the first time. 'I have been waiting for you,' she says to him.

XII

It is in these words that I recognize the 'You, you!', uttered by the woman in Toulouse, who has grown older, and yet who remains untrammelled by age, caught in the timelessness of desire; and who suddenly sees before her this person whom she had given up waiting for. Why this interest of mine, for *The Red Sands*? Because in the girl who emerged from a remote and endangered past, holding in her hands a prohibition that was also an invitation, I could already see the girl coming into the room with white walls but this time with a red scarf, a room where her future would be decided. Cepheis, the Roman, was my mother, glimpsed at the instant she would put an end to metaphysical maidenhood: by which I mean her relation to the world and to others ahead of the choices that necessarily shape a destiny.

And if I saw Cepheis in this way, it is because at the time I read the story, I understood already—not consciously, of course, and it would take me a long time, alas, fully to do so—that I was similarly expected, less by my mother in what was then her existence, but rather by the girl she was before, who had appeared at the threshold of her childhood house, not knowing who she was going to see, or what decision she would take. I felt that she awaited me, with the deepest, the most primal and intense desire, but at the same time I feared, reading *The Red Sands*, that I should not know how to respond.

As I reread *The Red Sands* today, I note that in a story where Cepheis is the only woman—only one other is seen, in the underground city, who says nothing, her face 'marked by sadness'—is less the acknowledgement by the son, insisted upon as it is, of the very masculine qualities belonging to an archaeologist devoted to his scientific research, than an indictment against him: the father accepts nothing that is not scientifically proven, and he steadfastly refuses to believe in the existence of these Romans, even as he pillages their goblets and amphoras. He believes not a word of the conversations with Cepheis that the 'young boy' describes. A total lack of understanding develops between the two of them, as the father's truth is nothing of the kind for the son, though the latter never seems to note—or want to understand—that here is matter for thought, and even for debate.

'You, you', the eternal girl had said, before a wall collapses between her and the one she waits for, as another one had, at the limit of the city she had just left, fallen and obliterated all trace of the queen of the red sands. 'You, you'— here is indeed matter for thought. Had I contributed, in one way or another, to the eviction of my father, if not from Hélène's heart, then certainly from her thoughts? The scarf that she held, was it to me and not to Elie that she offered it? It was the desire of the girl she had been, still in the unmediated intensity of childhood, that I had accepted to take upon me; and in this I acquiesced also in becoming like her father, Auguste Maury, the cause of Elie's banishment, that I deplored. Certainly I liked what I was becoming, my imagination brimming over as I launched into reading, discovering thoughts and worlds of which Elie had no notion.

Disturbing questions, assuredly. They have me searching my memory, here on this night train that goes thundering through vaulted tunnels—that revive 'ancient fears'—and heading towards what, I really still don't know. Who do I truly want to find at Toulouse? The stranger who had left his address on an empty envelope? Or the girl who had come into the room shortly before nightfall? Oh, '*vanne a Tolosa, ballatteta mia*'! Fly thence, my thoughts! Since I must ask why and whether, truly, leaving it between her hands, devoted to her alone,

> *Questo cor mi fu morto*
> *Poi che'n Tolosa fui.*

A Spelling Book

I

I have spoken of my father's silence, and of how it perturbed me when I was a child. But now I must enquire into another. For my mother, Hélène, was also silent.

Not in the ordinary way, by ceasing to speak. Hélène was by nature affable, interested in the people around her, beyond the family circle but not extending to society in general—the great matters of the age, some of them of major historical significance— did not much engage her. She undertook to share things with her neighbours, always with cheerfulness and good will. When she was on replacement duty, the other teachers looked down on her because she did not hold a permanent post, but she would affect not to notice and remained friendly and talkative, which won some of them over. People appreciated the genuine interest she took in others. They appreciated her courage.

At home with her children and her husband, she was talkative too, but she never spoke—in front of her son and daughter at least—of anything weighty. I cannot recall a single conversation concerning morality or politics, nor even about my own aspirations, my projects, or how I lived or what I did when I wasn't there, first at school, and later in Paris after I had gone there to live. My mother left all such matters to my own judgement, however uncertain or uninformed it might have been. Occasionally she would make an allusion that showed that she did worry, but it was always brief.

Was it due to lack of thought, or even to frivolity, that she chattered away outside, when within her immediate family circle she had this habit of closing down any discussion of wider existential import? To my mind, this was not the case, which is why I can speak of a silence. Very early on I perceived that this evasive woman was held at a deeper level than ordinary speech by thoughts and experiences she could not share, by words she did not want to compromise and even by hopes that she could scarcely admit to herself. There was a hermetically sealed space in her mind, and she deployed her chatter at home or in society as a defence mechanism. Proof of this place's reality, and of her eagerness to keep it hidden, would be the very abrupt way she would cut her children short when they started to talk about certain matters. In another text, I have already evoked the word *batchine*, used at one of those moments, that definitively put an end to any allusions to sexuality.[9]

9 In his volume, *Le Cœur-espace 1945, 1961* Bonnefoy explains in greater detail the word *batchine*, which derives from the Occitan patois used by his mother 'to cut short all discussion, all consideration of the possible merits of any matter she deemed it legitimate to proscribe'. Probably used by her own parents, and received by her as a stinging rebuke in her adolescence, the strange word resounded for the young Bonnefoy to similar effect: 'it resonated within me with more authority than any argument, precept or principle known to ordinary speech' (Tours: Editions Farrago, 2001, p. 46) .

What this carefully silenced thought was, that was kept from the speech of others, I understood very early on, for where words do not reveal, there are gestures, ways of reacting, of stalling, that betray it, for children, who are spontaneously attentive, are much more receptive than adults to these tiny signs. All it took was for her voice to tremble when she uttered certain names, or her hand tightening against mine when, on arrival at Toirac, she would open the little gate into the yard. We would leave our luggage in the thick, fragrant grass in front of the door, and only after this first moment return to collect it.

At moments like that, Hélène's secret, the memory that made her speech silent, was easy enough to guess; it centred on her attachment to the places and lifestyle of her childhood, to her father, and to episodes of her life as an adolescent that were perhaps too intimate and sometimes too painful to be shared with others. They would then, in her suffering mind, take on an additional reality. In Tours, and in many moments of her life as she had to live, my mother was an exile. Even though she repressed her tears so fiercely she seemed incapable of releasing them on any occasion, it was she I saw when I read in 'Ode to a Nightingale' how Keats, that great poet, describes Ruth, in tears among the sheaves of 'alien corn'.

She had already felt an exile with her young husband, which tempered, I imagine, during those early years, the feeling that must have awoken in her at the time of her first painful departure from Ambeyrac for the nursing school, leaving behind her bewildered parents, as she'd assumed them to be in her wounded and anxious pride; I can imagine her leaving abruptly, without looking back, in the same way that she and Elie would respond without hesitation to the added workload imposed by the war.

But soon after that early period came the events I have already described, the happy and unexpected removal of Hélène's parents to Toirac, the holiday visits there each summer, that stirred so many memories for the daughter, while at Tours the husband was soon to fall ill, darkening the future, and adding to the difficulties the couple already encountered. Unlike his wife, Elie had no parents or old friends remaining. At Viazac, as both his parents had died, we didn't go there any more, and at Toirac he felt insignificant, even an intruder. So much so that Hélène could no longer confide in him her dearest thoughts, even though she could see he suffered from feeling like an outsider, seeking clumsily for access to a world that to her was still bursting with life.

This disparity caused solitude, for him and for her, and my mother, closed in upon herself, must have ruminated all the more on what she had loved and lost, the child's being in the world, immediacy and presence. So she withdrew, just a little, from the alliance contracted twenty years earlier, and this is why it worries me when I read in my poem that the man from Toulouse thinks that it is upon me the scarf is draped, the scarf which represents, for the girl who has entered the room, recognition of the other and the giving of herself. Clearly he perceived soon enough her relative disenchantment with him.

II

Before my own birth, my mother had never experienced bringing up a child from infancy. Suzanne, her daughter, was born on 2 August 1914, the day before France entered the war; and almost from the beginning, given the influx of wounded soldiers and pressure on arms production, she was entrusted to the care of the grandparents in Viazac, where my sister spent the next four years. From this period and from the attachments she formed then, I think I can say in passing that she never returned to Tours entirely as Hélène's daughter. Did she resent having been left to others at the start of her life, did she identify more naturally with her father who was from Viazac, where they must often have spoken to her about him? Whatever the reason, I do not think that this very dutiful daughter, as she unfailingly was, really liked her mother. And that she lived deprived of the kind of attachment that is at the source of self-confidence later on, since it is intimately bound up with that early trust in someone else.

But Hélène was deprived in a way different from her daughter, although she herself was not at leisure to recognize the fact: she had no access, during those years, to the child's speech, with its profound link to the simplest of realities. She had already deprived herself, almost consciously or at least voluntarily, of the words that utter immediacy, once before: electing to become a nurse was to dedicate herself to the world of adults, dealing with lives and even bodies in states of medical emergency that made of them simply objects, mere matter almost. The world became reified into a discourse that, as the saying goes, called things by their names, scarcely leaving place for a disposition that can attend to their being, and which can thus keep the memories of childhood years alive.

For all that, whether in the infirmary at Bordeaux or in the overcrowded hospitals of 1914, the memories did not slip away, their recovery was merely stifled, her words yearning to recover their denotative capacity that the little child exercises so spontaneously, awakening an equivalent speech in the mother bent over him. Viewed from this angle, Suzanne had been a serious lost opportunity.

Anyway, the years went by, the war ended, Hélène stopped being a nurse, a little leisure time became available, there were brief excursions by train, with Elie, to the Châteaux of the Loire, or evenings in the garden of the new house near the railway workshops. And when, nine years after her first child, Hélène became a mother again, I think that this time she seized the opportunity thus offered. My mother found the time to listen to my first words, to answer with the same words or others like them, and also to speak to the children who came up to us in the Prébendes d'Oé, the public garden. There were screams, exclamations, denotative words, and through them the capacity to capture things in the immediacy of the emotion they provoked, the desires, and for Hélène it was to reconnect with her early years, and to release the flood of memories stored there. Her father, as he was then, also reappeared, and her childhood home opened up. Hélène could ascend the stairs, and look at the beautiful countryside through the windows: all this was the resource she could not share with her husband, but that she sensed she could with me, who was of her own blood.

The words of a young child in effect allowed the young woman who heard and spoke them with me to return to the never-forgotten intensity of her origins. And I believe it was this reconnection that led my mother, a few years later, to teach me to read. It may seem natural for a schoolteacher to want to instruct her own son, rather than to leave the task to someone else; but I feel that in her case this went beyond the usual possessive instinct. I can see before me now, on the dining table where meals were served after the hour of instruction, an ABC, a tall thin book, with worn, greenish covers; this contained the images that were, page after page, framed by a magnificent capital letter. Here were images of a cat for the letter 'C', or of a house fringed by trees for the letter 'H'. Succinct and boldly coloured, these were line drawings that had no use for dictionary definitions, they were destined simply to show a cat or a house or a tree to the child bent over the book. And the child would relive through them what belongs innately to being in the world, while at the same time discovering the existence of trees, of trees in general, but also of becoming attached to a familiar tree, and to feel it as a friendly presence.

An understanding, both of the species, grasped before any further reaching after conceptualization, but also of the particular being, as it can be apprehended in an instant and in a place. These images were thus archetypes and not illustrations. They evoked the constituent parts of a place on earth, of a home, not at all exempla in a system of knowledge. It was also an evocation that might seem poor, but that very poverty, in the schematic drawing, left ajar beneath its disjointed lines a sort of space that let in light. The grace of these drawings was that the visible was punctured all over by the invisible, as though the surface of some underlying unity of everything were lightly brushed—it is of this that the ABC spoke, though only accessible to those not yet enjoined to the viewpoint and project of analytic knowledge. I was thus invited to remain faithful to the first way in which we use words—to their denotative and exclamatory functions. So I came to learn of two levels of discourse. And I had access, below the articulations of the conceptual, to a deeper source, to being itself, using the vocables of a language at the heart of a language that are the ones religions refer to when they speak of the *logos*.

I have just summarized in abstract if not hermetic terms what I lived through, without of course understanding it explicitly, when I pored over my ABC. But I did so the better to understand what was going on in the still-hopeful woman who initiated me into this language, this gatherer-together of a world coming apart, this Isis of the little house by the railway line. By revealing to me the great power stored in a few simple words, my mother inspired me, in my future life, not to give up on the child's gaze, which had helped her in her own existence to find her feet again. She called upon me to accept from her the red scarf, which was hers to offer at a crucial moment in her life: that piece of cloth within whose folds the world still seemed steeped in being, in unity, in that which gives meaning to life.

And the scarf was her blood, also, it was of Ambeyrac and not of the other place with its harsher landscape, Viazac, where my father did not remain a child happy enough or for long enough to remember the riches of this inaugural state of being. This explains, in my view, what happened later on between Elie and Hélène, and also my relationship with them. I felt called upon, in the life before me, to preserve a use of words of which my father felt incapable. I would speak this more vigilant language, and he would merely perceive its bizarre exterior, which led to him feeling still more confined to the wretched exchanges in the factory, the daily grind and the newspaper he would try to read when he got home in the evening.

III

It was his misfortune, then, that I was able to respond to the call, and to devote myself to what I might call the poetic use of language. Was this simply due to the impact upon me of those welcoming images in the big book? Or from impressions I received even earlier? In any case, I have always loved in words the promise they give of a higher level of reality than commonly experienced. People told me, at school or at the bookseller's, to get interested in the thoughts and plans of the boy in this book, written for people your age, but the boy in question, nearly an adolescent, was quite alien to me, along with his needs and actions. But when I read—and these are the opening words of a story published by the same firm as *The Red Sands*: ' "Ireland is a delightful country!" exclaimed Eric in a hoarse voice'—this phrase dazzled me, and eagerly I set foot upon the land of the absolute, where even that word 'hoarse' was a mystery, when I felt what Rimbaud called '*épouvante*'—a shudder.

My interest for words was sharp, and sharpened further, when the texts I read were not fully clear to me—if they were, it would have brought me back to my own daily existence: and I was soon reading Racine, though I could scarcely understand who Phèdre was, or the feelings that tormented her. What she said was enough: '*Mes yeux sont éblouis du jour que je revois.*'[10] The rhythm too, with that scansion which

10 'My eyes are dazzled by the day I recall' (Jean Racine, *Phèdre*, Act I, Scene 3, 1677).

rises within language as something deeper within it than the surface meaning, this rhythm was a kind of threshold to me, a pathway, and it attached me to poems of no great value but whose facile alexandrines threw into relief nouns, and even adjectives: '*La grande plaine est blanche, immobile et sans voix*',[11] I would read, and repeat: and how extraordinary, how 'out of the world' was that whiteness, that stillness, that silence! I loved poems, even wretched ones, and I would write my own of course, in my thirst to wrest language away from what it was in my milieu, so that within the family, at Tours, but also at Toirac, I was known as a poet. 'Future Poet', wrote my aunt Lucie, who was my godmother as well, in a collection of poems she inscribed for me on, I believe, my ninth birthday.

People would call me that in the family, even at home, when we would lay the table for supper, and this was why I was distressed to read in *The Red Scarf* that what I knew and would not admit: that I had in fact contributed—unintentionally, of course—to the sadness and isolation of my father. A manual worker himself, he saw in me a future foreman or even an engineer, and there I was with my strange interests, a book of poems, a notebook in which I had sketched out a tragedy, things that carried me off he knew not where and turned me into someone he could not recognize. Elie's curtailed childhood was such that he could not understand what was taking shape in my own.

11 'The wide plain is white, motionless and without voice' (Guy de Maupassant, 'Nuit de neige', *Des vers,* 1908).

And for my part, I now feel that I was nevertheless at fault. Taken up by words, and their promise of another world, I did not need, or really need my father, and I did not seek his attention in a way that would have benefited him. Much later, I reflected on this, as a kind of apologia, in *The Curved Planks*; on what a son may owe to a father, who comes to him, sometimes clumsy, always shy, outside the *hortus conclusus* of the relation with the mother. What must the child, still at the heart of plenitude, of a world of presence, offer an adult already exiled from this world by his conceptualized words? Cry out to him that he is but a little being who needs to be gathered up by strong arms and swept laughing off the ground in a moment of suffocating intimacy. This kind of game gives a weary and careworn man the chance to grow young again, and recover in his depths what was dormant but still alive, the ability to welcome the trusting joy of another being. A welcome that instantly banishes uneasiness as well, shedding light everywhere on his relation to his own inner self.

And now as I think of it, today, I realize there were never any games with my father; he never ran with me, never laughed or shouted. I can recall sharing only one instance of intimacy with him: it was when I was ill, with measles, and in bed; on the coverlet were one or two toys, and those oranges wrapped in the clear paper one often liked to unfold, flatten and smooth out. My father returned from work, and came and sat near the bed, and remained there for a long while, in silence. I believe that he was asking me to ask, and because I never did, thanks to my obsession with words, I did him an injustice. My manifest interest in words other than his would combine with Hélène's new distraction to reduce him to that silence which worried me, being unable to understand its nature.

A Painting by Max Ernst

I

Given the nature of my growing vocation, I can only conclude therefore that it contributed to the feeling of solitude that Elie, my father, experienced in his latter years. But does it necessarily follow that I let him down in some way? In actual fact, given my later rather ambivalent attitude to words, one that contained affection, but also a wariness concerning them—a resource but also a lure—I remained in a way, belatedly alas, close to him. My principal idea concerning poetry, which I believe is fundamentally sound—based on the inherent contradiction that stimulates it—I owe undoubtedly to him.

What did I do, in the years after his early death? First of all I became intoxicated with words, I wallowed in their mixed lights and shades, I fashioned my dreams out of them, and imagined that through them I could attain a more intense reality than that afforded me by this world. For a long time I remained, and at times I still am, imprisoned by this snare. And it was this that for a long time founded my belief that a consciousness more attuned to this higher absolute must have become established somewhere on this earth, and by this token, removed from other societies; and that in this country just shy of our own, perhaps a couple of steps away from where we are, a higher and more satisfying spiritual order and activity had held sway. Toirac, as I had experienced it under the tutelage of my mother, was a contributing cause of this mirage.

But well before these thoughts, in my own childhood, I had already lived through experiences and emotions of quite another nature. They were made up of instants, not the vague and floating time of dream. It was also in the here and now, where I was, and not yet where words called to me, beyond the horizon of the known world. And the context was all very ordinary, in the most familiar of settings, but added to them was a kind of standing forth—*surgissement*—that obliterated material reality: suddenly these events, these things, were nothing but the incomprehensible act of their being raised before me.

In various earlier essays or in poems I have already evoked some of these instants, have in fact been obliged to do so and to return to them because they are my deepest memory. And now I must refer to them once again, but this time in a context that enables me better to understand them. For example there was an isolated tree on the crest of a hill two or three kilometres distant from the house in Toirac. I would often gaze with this longing for an elsewhere, at the long ridge with its stones, its straggling bushes; and suddenly the tree imprinted itself on me, not as a part of a place I found beautiful but as a being that stood forth, almost effacing the rest, to cry out, in its solitude, the fact of its existence:

it was there, in the here and now, it might not have been here, one day it wouldn't be, and its presence was therefore to be lived as an enigma, a mystery even, and it required that I should let it resonate to my depths, exchanging my view of it from a simple thing to one that would fathom an abyss below outer appearance.

Another time, during those same years and in that same country, the song of one bird came clear of the others to address me, though it still consisted of its set notes: the sound had become filled with the invisible, and yet remained what it was, except that once again it was no longer anything other than the trace of an enigma, the same enigma, in the devastated space where existence had been. I could describe it as a voice, a hoarse voice emerging from what was now the entirely external beauty of the world.

But the most striking of all these experiences, and the one which guided my consequent thinking about works of art, be it poetry, painting or sculpture, was this: night had fallen, we were returning from the nearby farm with fresh milk, and coming by the first house at the entrance to the village, there was a window open and a lamp burning within. And suddenly there I saw, all at once, a black silhouette against the light, a man standing, bent over some task or other. What a shock! A perception of the fact of being, and with it the fear of non-being, and to feel oneself swept towards a stranger by the surge of solidarity in the heart of an absolute, vertiginous solitude, only now fully grasped!

That man, framed in his window not of this world, was not one of the beings who spoke to me in my ABC, with its archetypal images: but these were living beings too, not just things, and I had a veritable experiential relation with them. For the houses and animals and men and women in the book were on my side, so to speak, in my task of putting together the world; they were available to my desires, malleable to them, and richly clothed in the best of my perceptions whereas that other existence, in the lit window, came from without, was irreducibly other, utterly strange, a question without an answer. No longer some imagined plenitude at the heart of some other place I might perhaps accede to one day, but steps giving way beneath my feet.

II

I had had an experience of nothingness, a scare, and after it I looked at the things around me with different eyes. What there was, in those moments, was no longer the world as expressed in nature, in its numberless creatures, but rather something without body, reference points, or even the slightest proof of its existence, this standing forth, which is nothing else, in and of itself, than total solitude, an infinite vulnerability. I assume this is a common enough experience, even if most often repressed. Every child knows of this—it lies behind their night-time fears and is the reason they want to hear stories before bed. But for me it was also, as I now see, a memory of my father when he came to sit in silence beside my bed.

For many years after this, it lay dormant within me, a cause of bad dreams. Adolescence is distraction, or tries to be, and it was so for me, my words—my verses—flowing around the memory of that night window.

But my sense of non-being awoke when, at the age of sixteen or seventeen, I first encountered the images and writings of the Surrealists. André Breton's exalted exhortation to 'change life' enthused many of us in those years at the end of the war, and I tried to do just that. But in fact what drew me to Surrealism was its dark side, its very real shadowy slope sitting just next to its utopian sunny upland. More specifically I was drawn to Max Ernst's infinitely black hills, inherited from Dada and foreshadowing what Breton called the 'object'.

The object, the surreal object? Aspects of the most ordinary reality, but assembled in the most heterogeneous and contradictory manner, in a montage that enters unreality, an image untenable in this world, but made up of existences close to it, on the threshold of our reality, asking in silence to be received. Like those hands clasped around nothingness in Giacometti's *Invisible Object*, the epiphany of some impossible otherness that transgresses the laws of nature and points towards an unknowable and terrifying future. The loftiest and most intense realization of this intuition was realized in the collages of Max Ernst, in particular his series *Semaine de bonté*, in the folds of whose implacable incomprehensibility Ernst observed what had been revealed to me in that nocturnal window in Toirac. Surrealism, that dream of superabundant being, is at bottom in fact animated by an apprehension of nothingness, which is very strong and very compelling. Breton knew as much, which is why his writing has such power, even if it seems, on the surface, tentative.

Max Ernst and Giacometti reminded me therefore of what I had tried to forget, and they required of me that I should give up the words of my ABC, which I imbibed like opium. Faced with Ernst's divinities, made of every shade of darkness and admitted into the here and now, the images of that diurnal world—possessed of riches though they were—the trees and rivers that I loved, were revealed as nothing but images, destined to veil the terrors of the abyss.

This came as a big shock to me, of course. I understood that what sustains the desire for beings and things as he envisions them—I mean in their entirety, in their presence, and the way they suggest an underlying unity of all things—depends after all on certain of their aspects only, at the expense of others: and this in fact substitutes for the full flood of presence a simple montage of these aspects, a representation as dangerous, if not poisonous, for the intellect and the emotional life as scientifically orientated thought. The imagination too is a conceptualization, and the realm of the *imaginaire* is as much a creation of schemas and models as are the hypotheses and formulations of science; its abstractions belong to another type of discourse, simply that of myth, foreign to the research of the physicist or the sociologist but similarly forgetful—or in denial—of the finitude of the realities evoked. It follows that the poems which wander abstractedly—*rêveusement*—among words, plucking them out, so to speak, at their pleasure—well, one has to conclude that such poems evade the challenge laid down by the abyss.

I need to add however that this perception of the dream world, as lacking in reality—or lacking in the ideas that constitutes oneself—did not in any way, when I engaged in it, diminish my faith in the possibility of a life in the here and now, endowed with being; on the contrary I felt that it set me on the right path. In a piece I wrote at that time, I find the notion of a 'black hygiene' from which I expected 'everything', or so I said, I expected that 'change of life'.

What then was this resource? I shall try and explain.

III

And to do so we need to refer to Max Ernst again, this time to one of his paintings, a work that is famous today but that for a long time was familiar only to readers of Surrealist publications. The instant I saw it, I do not recall in which journal, I was fascinated by his *Pietà*, also called *La Révolution la nuit* (Revolution by Night). So much so that I adopted these four words as the title for my own little review, which I wanted to found and which did, in fact, appear, as two slim pamphlets littered with confusions.[12] Clearly certain elements of the painting were useful to me in my reflections on poetry, but probably even more for the work I needed to do on myself. But of course I was at that time unable to understand clearly what was starting to happen.

What is happening in *La Révolution la nuit*, a painting that one might at first consider as a still in a film recounting the evening after a riot? The mustachioed man in the bowler hat does seem to be one of the policemen, some of them in civilian dress, who beat the demonstrators with their truncheons: there is a wounded man, with a bandaged head, against the wall of a nearby building. But now he is holding another man on his lap, a very young man, who could have been knocked unconscious. Nothing could be more natural than to read into this scene, for all its mystery, an association with the desire for social revolution that began to stir in the Surrealist group in the 1920s: to transform life meant first of all to put an end to the exploitation of the proletariat, and that entailed demonstrations in the street, inventing and spreading slogans, and violence, inflicted and suffered, in preparation for the revolution.

12 The first issue of this pro-Surrealist 'brulôt' (polemical tract) was published in 1946 when the poet was twenty-three and contains, among other things, six propositions by Bonnefoy under the title 'La Nouvelle Objectivité'; the first reads, in keeping with one of the eternal paradoxes of the poet's later thought and practice: 'Every dogmatist is an assassin. Every metaphysician, a robber of corpses' (*Traité du pianiste et autres écrits anciens*, Paris: Mercure de France, 2008, pp. 129–34).

But it is also at the level of the image that one can invest it with bad memories for a young person looking at it, still raw from the Oedipal stage of his existence. The man in suit and tie is clearly a father, who is holding his son in his arms, and the way one dominates the other is the father, crushing the son's freedom, and for Max Ernst it was the struggle against his own father, which was apparently an attested fact. It is easy to apply a Freudian interpretation and it does seem justified here, linking up as it does with the political reading, with its suggestion that the thirst for social revolution contains within it an Oedipal situation that, while not the cause itself, certainly nourishes it.

But should I see in *La Révolution la nuit* merely this aspect of the narrative? What in fact leaps out of the painting is the contrast between the way the background scene and the putative policeman is painted, and on the other hand the treatment accorded to the young man, the putative victim. It is dark, the city and the street are poorly lit, the man in the suit does not stand out from the ambient darkness that broods on the world, a world in which the meaning of colour has no place. The young man, by contrast, is all brilliant colour and light, a white and a red in the foreground of the painting, so intense and violently autonomous that they seem forcefully to cancel out the more pessimistic tones further back. Colour, repressed, has reappeared, and it rescues from nothingness the figure it clothes, or even from whom it emanates.

There is no question that Max Ernst sought this contrast, and he wanted to invest it with meaning. And the meaning he wanted might seem obvious, the darkness in the painting signifying existence in a world as alienated as it is unjust, to be pulled down, and colour—the white, the red, and even a hint of blue in the background shadow—constitutes the flag that would carry the necessary revolution, the flame of this new hope. As for the young man's appearance, it speaks of what Surrealism intends to nurture at the heart of the revolutionary project, the role that subjectivity must play, and its contribution, held to be irreplaceable, to the means and ends of 'changing life'. This being, who is less carried than raised, or presented—is he really inanimate? No, if he is immobile, he is so without recoil or suffering, and in fact he is asleep, his eyes both open and closed, in an active gaze, and he is dreaming. Dreamwork, and the vigilance of the unconscious lie behind these colours and this light, for it is they who must guide the militant revolutionary, preceding the serious action to come, which is recognizable as a sister force.

IV

It is easy enough to decipher the meaning of Max Ernst's painting, so completely in accord with Surrealist thinking; and the message I duly received contributed to my fascination for the picture. But I know full well that there was another level to this fascination.

It is so striking—the complexity and even the ambiguity of the relationship between the young man in the foreground, in full colour, and the other who seems to be carrying him, in shadow! Is he carrying him, is he bearing him away? But no, he is on his knees, which brings the painting's other title to mind, *Pietà*, a word that refers to those paintings and sculptures in which the Virgin expresses her grief, hunched over the body of the dead god, often holding him in her arms. It is easy enough to see the personage in the bowler hat as a repressive figure, but it is equally possible to see in him a meditative one who has compassion or even respect for the being he clasps tight, in the manner of the Virgin: and the expression on his face—the eyes closed, veiling the gaze, the slight smile—does nothing to counter this hypothesis. Does the smile seem unreadable? But one has only to remember the perplexity of little children faced with the behaviour or the expressions of grown-ups.

To the conflicted relation between father and son, Max Ernst's painting adds, or substitutes, what might be at the very least intimacy, and on the part of the father even affection or a repressed emotion, which contains hope. Who is this son that he holds in his arms? Is he someone whose strange sleep resembles death, even in the hours shared with him? Or is he a disconcerting being, whose unusual colour seems to be the promise in this occluded life of a reality higher than the present condition of things? The secret of this may be inaccessible, the opposition between the radiant apparel of this angel of the new ages and one's own sad clothing being so marked. But one has at least glimpsed it, which is cause for a little happiness.

These are, in any case, very different notions from those proposed by the Freudian understanding, which treats the relationship between father and son at a much more archaic level, before the mind is overwhelmed by the invasion of the conceptual with the consequent devastation of existence wrought by the discovery of death: and that includes the death, in the end, of those closest to us, the most loved, a discovery that brings to us the understanding that we have loved. Now, what struck me all at once in Ernst's painting, and entirely on the conscious level, was the resemblance between the man in jacket and bowler hat and my own father, Elie, when he got dressed for the obligatory constitutional on Sunday afternoons. This would be under a sunny sky, with nothing of the tangled shadows of a night of rioting—but the man in the middle ground nevertheless wore the same clothes as my father, and the same kind of silence about him, the same distance at the heart of his undeniable affection; above all he had the same features, the same moustache.

My father was resurrected, in *La Révolution la nuit*, or in *Pieta*, and he even brought another memory with him. One day, when still a little child, I had fallen down the stone stairs in the Toirac house, rolling down step by step, and it was my father, who had been following me, who gathered me up in his arms, but who also cried out in panic, 'My son is dead!' I was no more dead than the youth in the painting by Max Ernst, and indeed I heard his cry, which proved his affection for me. And I have just noticed, today, that there is a staircase at the bottom right corner of the painting.

How many things correspond, and coincide in this image, or this icon, with my personal anxiety! Painted in the year of my birth, it is as though it had waited for the day when I would really understand it—and that day had now come. It is not that I recognize in these figures and symbols the Oedipal relationship, composed of a mixture of attraction and hostility, but the perception of another ambiguity, proof of the affection of a father for a son who seems to refuse it, but also the presentiment that as far as the latter is concerned, who is perhaps not as closed off as it appears, there is a process at work, still unconscious, but which one day—the colour proclaims it so—would be benign.

Let me put this another way. I am engaged in a process whose path is clear, even if strewn with innumerable obstacles. I shall decide that the other, even though only ever perceived in dream is—on its foundations of cloud, being itself—the only one there is. It *is*, and I am with it, the chance place we share is also *is*, and it appears before my eyes with its hills, trees, the pathways in the clearing mist. And I discover that all this has a truth, and thus a beauty, which the dream had veiled, and fed on at the same time. And thus it is that our task, from childhood on, by using the great words in the language that let in the light, to strip away as far as possible the reveries with their images that deprive us of what is there, not by repressing its drives but by revealing the reasons for them, and their desire to have, eternally, this—which, through confining them to their own categories, prevents the mind from ranging into the universal for encounters that turn into recognitions. This is therefore a work of negation, but whose future gives way to presence.

There is thus a double postulation, which may be cause for alarm; it is a cleft, a schism, at work in all poems, at each instant of a poem, as it is at the heart of the human condition; that the creature with language uses conceptual thought, which deprives it of a grounding in finitude, and makes perpetual dreamers of us. Everyone, therefore, is called to the task. We might call it a moral quest, and it is in fact an ontological one because it involves a creation of the world, a creation that is continued.

I began to apprehend all this with *La Révolution la nuit.* A conception of poetry that considers poetry to be a form of exchange. It was 1946. My father, had he lived, would not even have been sixty years old.

The Silent Third

I

If I have digressed at length, relating my years of apprentice-ship, it has enabled me to make peace, so to speak, with the growing anxiety that I have also described in some detail. But I now consider myself authorized to understand that disap-pointing an expectation is not necessarily a fault. Or rather, that it is something reparable. A presence has been betrayed, one has no memory of it at the crucial moments with the other person, but to reflect is to remember, when in conjunc-tion with the need to write. And I realize that from the moment I became involved with Surrealism, this thought was constantly borne by me, under the rubric of to be or not to be, as that question is asked on the 'dark' side of André Breton's project. It was then that I set myself presence—among others, that of loved ones—as my own poetic project, and I tried to beat a track through the labyrinth of meanings that litter the task of writing, in which insights are so con-stantly displaced. As I reflected on poetry in the years fol-lowing my *Anti-Platon*, it may be that I had never in fact forgotten the man whose silence, full of sadness, had trig-gered my first thoughts on language.

My father, with his questioning, and what he expected from me, is present in the texture of my writings, once they ceased being just preparatory exercises. I did not mention him by name until late on in my life, but that does not imply that he was not always one of its preoccupations, the proof being this same 'Red Scarf', with the empty envelope and the man standing in the *contre-jour* of a window just like—as I realize now—the other man, between being and non-being, I had seen framed in a window, at night that time, and in Toirac.

I haven't forgotten . . . But have I not done just that, after all, this time in relation to the person who seemed so fully to occupy my thoughts? She who was also silent? I have spoken of my attachment to my mother's dream, and of our complicity in that. But had I ever understood the real nature of the desire behind it?

A memory comes back to me, as it does often, from the war years. From the village where my mother had since become a teacher, every day I would take the train to the school in Tours; it was early in the morning, it was winter and still dark, but I did not linger in the waiting room, I crossed the double tracks to wait on my own, on the other side, under the little shelter, for the local train that would emerge from the mysterious region of the Grand Meaulnes.[13] That particular morning, the train which arrived from Tours,

13 When Bonnefoy was in his early teens, his widowed mother moved to the village of Saint Martin le Beau, among the vineyards above Amboise. The train would be coming from Blois, Chambord, and beyond that, the Sologne.

which usually passed my train some way before our station, was a little delayed, and it had only just started moving again, when in a great flurry of steam and noise the locomotive pulling my own train, still moving fast, swept in. Between the train that was leaving and the great fracas of that arriving, for one second the other side of the platform, from where I had just come, was visible. And what did I see, about to go under the wheels of the locomotive coming in, but violently thrust back by the platform master who, ashen-faced, with a yell, hurled himself forward to save her? My mother, Hélène, just a few centimetres clear of the great wheels that would have crushed her! I clambered up through the nearest door, dashed over to the one opposite, and lowered the window: there was my mother, at the foot of the coach, stretching out towards me, not a scarf, but handkerchiefs. She knew that I had a cold, she'd noticed after I left that I had forgotten them, so she had run to the station.

II

An instant before the blind mass and the sound of the train, that vision of her face paralysed with terror! I can never remember that instant without it bringing to mind the other one, when I had seen her, this time on the pavement in front of the house, waiting for me to return from school, after the death of my father. And as I think back now, there comes to my mind the end of *The Red Scarf*, when the woman appears on another threshold and exclaims, 'You, you!', and then again in a moment marked by urgency, illness and death. What was it, this secret of Hélène's? Dream, the withdrawal of life into representations, into fixed memories, of Ambeyrac, of Toirac? Yes, but also a very strong instinct that took her towards beings that existed outside her dream: a refocusing of thought, and of action, on to this outside, on to this absolute.

That morning, I understood that my mother lived not only in denial of her current circumstances, in a way that encouraged me also to inhabit worlds made out of my words: she was attached to existence in the here and now, and in fact, by trying to get to me before my train arrived, she made of it an absolute priority, at the risk of her life. It was a gift she gave to me, a world new-born, but it was also a request: in her remaining years she needed to be recognized, she required the attention of her loved ones. As much as she'd needed Elie in his day, she now needed me. This is clear from the way she waited for me on the pavement, only a few minutes after my father died. And it cries out in *The Red Scarf* with that 'You, you!' on another threshold, an expression of hope.

I ought to have understood. When I experienced this surge within me of affection and anxiety for the woman I watched ageing, distant now from her springtime, from the girl who had entered the room. I should have understood, and very nearly I did. But I still remained, in those years, the boy that, entering a compartment of the train that came from somewhere out of his life—coming from an absolute elsewhere—would sit down with a book in his hands that spoke to him, or had him speak, of that hidden country. From one end to the other of the coach were the men and women who had become over the months and years, familiar faces without ever becoming known. Right next to me was a pretty girl who seemed ready to talk, and whose serious, grave face I liked, and yet I took care to keep her at a distance: she came from further up the line than I, she came from that mysterious upstream, from the heart of some transcendence, how could she ever descend from that higher world? With a name to follow, and a life among other lives! I preferred to take from my satchel the *Poèmes* of Paul Valéry which I had at last obtained from the ignorant bookseller, and take up my reading of the 'Fragments du Narcisse', or of the 'Cantique des colonnes', by means of which I acceded directly to my heart's desire. And I continued with my dreaming, and remained in a state of latency.

III

Yet it is not that the other way of looking—which is attached to the here and now, to the reality of the near at hand—did not begin to open my eyes, under the impact of the works of Max Ernst that I have just spoken of. A young philosophy teacher, who was in fact just a replacement, without the usual qualifications, had come to Tours in the chaos of the return to school in October 1940, and he immediately won my sympathy, inspiring in me a vibrant if still vague kind of hope;

to get his attention, on one of the first days he was among us, I wrote in chalk on the blackboard before he came in: '*La voix des sources change et me parle du soir*',[14] a line made of gleams and shadows that seemed to be deep as an abyss. Of course, the moment he arrived, standing in front of the rowdy class, he exclaimed, 'Who wrote that?', which marked the beginning of a personal friendship that prompted him to show and lend me books by Surrealist writers that he had brought with him from Paris. Valéry's poetics, in a dialectical opposition— a dream under the rule of the intellect, a very controlled, but unbounded, daytime reverie, and a triumphant one—would falter in the maze of automatic writing, and the adherence to strict form and constraint would fall away, in a recognition of the reality and the truth of chance. The Surrealist books, with their dissonant voices, and their disturbing images, set me on the right path. But it was to be a long journey.

For my thought about the other world persisted and came clear, I have spoken of it already, in how light—'*si seulement il faisait du soleil cette nuit*'[15] which I had read in *Clair de terre*— created a darkness made of cries and yelps in the intuitions of Ernst, Breton, Giacometti and Victor Brauner, while at the same instant these others, these poets and painters became for me the inhabitants of a world that was

14 'The voice of the streams changes and speaks to me of evening' (Paul Valéry, 'Fragments du Narcisse', *Charmes*, 1922).
15 'If only the sun would shine tonight' (André Breton, *Clair de terre*, 1923).

entirely discontinuous with ours: Paris perhaps, but only certain crossroads known to an select few, the routes to which were lost in a maze of streets. So it was not my troubled adherence to the Imperatives of the Surrealist group, as they were around 1930, which stopped me for some years yet from transfiguring reality at the cost of occasions and encounters. The unconscious tried hard to find a way out, as I believe it always will, even from its worst illusions, but in my case it was no easy task, and the period of latency, and a burdening of the mind, went on, persisted—it had merely changed the matter of its reverie.

IV

I would return home, sometimes every evening, and sometimes only at the weekends, with books that exploited my preoccupation, and carried me off in directions that seemed to give weight to this idea of the Surreal, which I did not then realize had blinded *Nadja* and the allegiances in *Pas perdus*, or in *Point du jour*, that were my bibles at the time.[16]

16 Bonnefoy cites here three key texts by Breton, *Les Pas perdus* (1924), *Nadja* (1928), and *Point du jour* (1934). The first and the last are composed of critical essays, while *Nadja* recounts the real-life meeting with a young woman whom Breton later discovered to be a psychiatric patient. All three texts dwell on the Surrealist notion of 'objective chance' which is essentially the belief that somewhere 'out there' in the world exist certain objects that are already existing embodiments of our inner desires, they just need to be found, in 'privileged encounters', a dependency that Bonnefoy later came to reject.

I had interests elsewhere too; in the philosophy of science, I discovered Bachelard, I pondered what he called the Surrational, and whether it could be linked to Breton's Surreal and what it promised me. And today I can only declare that I lost an opportunity with regards to my relationship with my mother, during those years that were in fact everywhere so dark for society and for the world.

I would leave early in the morning, often while it was still dark, but invariably Hélène had long been up and hard at work, getting the fire going again, chopping wood, drawing water from the pump, feeding the hens and rabbits that constituted the wartime sustenance at the far end of a narrow, noisy courtyard. The lack of comfort in this house, which adjoined the town hall and the municipal clock, but also the farms in the neighbourhood, with their smells and noises, had awakened her ancestral habits and capacities: like her mother before her, she had a steady hand when, amid the smell of mint that grew wild all around, it came to cutting the throat of a hen or a rabbit, however they'd thrash about. And the vipers that infested the nearby fields turned her into a nurse again: someone would get bitten, they would call my mother, and she would rush out with her syringes and vaccine, crying out as she arrived at the door: 'Put some water on to boil!'

In the evening I would return for supper near the wood stove, still glowing red, and after we had eaten and cleared up, she would place on the table the school copybooks which she had to correct, along with the history or geography text books which she would need to consult, while I would sit opposite her, behind my own books that I had scarcely read. Sometimes she would reach out for one of these strange works, read a few lines and then close it, without saying a word. In a little while she would prepare the hot wine we drank to brace ourselves for the cold rooms upstairs. Was it always winter, during those war years? I am tempted to think so. In any case, France was cut in two, and Toirac existed only in the past, along with her sister Lucie, and indeed her whole childhood region was in the unoccupied zone. My mother was forced to remain here, in the coldest winters of the century, but she never stopped thinking about the other place, now barred to her.

I saw the woman I had known when she was young, or even say before time had begun, start to grow old. I saw her grow old and change, her little pupils, and their parents, and the responsibility for them she had taken on, along with the daily grind, preoccupied her more and more. I could already imagine her retirement, when she had moved back to Tours, a town with few happy memories for her, and how every afternoon she would go alone to the Prébendes garden or the garden in the Musée des Beaux Arts: just like one of the 'little old ladies' described by Baudelaire in the most moving of his great poems. Something harsh, also, and remote, had settled in her face, that made me think of the mother carved out of oak with 'strokes of the axe', as Tristan Corbière described the Saint Anne in the chapel at Auray.[17] That future filled me with horror, and I felt the preciousness of what was left in her of life, or even, of vivacity.

V

Why did I not take advantage of those two or three years, during which we hardly moved, to ask her questions, or pique her memory? Or ask her to go into herself, in order to help her to understand and resolve what it was that troubled her, when she went to sleep or when, after class, and to the astonishment of the village, she would go off and wander along the empty banks of the nearby river Cher? I might have been the interlocutor she needed, who could have restored some faith in herself, which had little by little been lost in the disappointments of her life. 'You, you!'—was that not the good she hoped for, after losing her husband—her son's attention?

But I did not then feel strongly enough the need for being that remains alive in the renunciation the dream brings with it; and instead of following the example of this woman who lingered by the banks of the Cher, which had to stand in for the Lot, I should have refused my own chimeras, having realized that they were analogous with her own, and tried to address her within the space of our shared existence, the hearth from where a flame could still spring forth from a few skilfully placed embers. The dream is what can separate,

17 See Tristan Corbière's poem 'Lar rapsode foraine et le pardon de Sainte-Anne' from *Les amours jaunes* (1873).

certainly, but it can also bring together when one understands, through the dismantling of one's own, what constitutes the other person's. It should then be possible to sit down with the other person, trying to simplify the desires, and to talk through the shared nostalgia and the memories, and the past and present of real life. An exchange, of the most serious import, because it takes place at the level where being in the world has leverage, and where its values have some chance of regaining colour and life. An exchange that has absolutely no need for abstract thought, for it can start with talk about the daily round, or by laying out old photographs on the table.

An exchange to engender being, being that is never anything other than a joining together. For it would restore this bruised existence back to the metaphysical purity that had invested all its lovely hope in the gift of a scarf, in its own way the preservation of what one could call the spirit of childhood, which gazes all around knowing and desiring nothing other than presence. A purity of soul that the giver of the red scarf could assuredly not countenance without grave risk; and much better therefore that she have around her beings who know the cost of her gesture. Who knew how to ask of the ABC not for a China or an India, but how to illuminate a hill, a house, and a few lives, gathered together for a while, within a thoughtful enveloping gaze.

It would seem that somewhere within me I desired this return to the denotative in words, which is why I have a memory of a mother and her son, in another children's book, running towards a station with a huge and menacing clock. Desiring the simple, the timeless, entails of course having to understand time's pledge, and to realize that it exists, hearing in the station down there, up there, the sound of an approaching train, that will rapidly be gone, a lost opportunity.

In the room with the deep recesses, I ought since I was there to have come forwards out of the shadow, when the visitor from Toulouse had left, in the hotel where he was living. To have come forward, to have understood the meaning of the scarf held out still, and to accept what was offered, I mean, to have spoken, and broken by means of words yet heedful of the need of the other, the established silence, and with it, its true inhibitions but also its strange distinctions between my parents, Elie and Hélène. To speak to the woman who had fallen silent and thereby, for a second, or even for a first time, restore her to the world. But I see very well that I was incapable of such a decisive action, and perhaps even today I can only dream of performing it. And I note, simply, the missed opportunity caused by this third silence.

It was a silence that lasted, too, and it was not to end in Hélène's lifetime. In fact I left my mother to her own muteness, having made of her dream one of the causes of my own— a dream that lasted a long time, and that did not dissipate, in so far as it did, until it was too late for her. What were those years like, in reality? I brooded, it's true, and I seemed to take some decisions—enshrined in my book *Anti-Platon* with its intuition of the goodness of the finite nature of things. But in the seasons before that poem, and in those that followed, the dream unfurled itself around that intuition, it drew upon and even turned it to its own profit: these were my reveries of fully realised presence, but existing elsewhere than here, unrealizable; I have described their nature and their tenacity in my book *The Arrière-pays*. The idea of the authentic place had to struggle for its life against the illusion of a 'true place', and that struggle was enacted in my first book of poems, before the acknowledgment of its failure—which was the beginning of the second volume—five years later.[18]

VI

I was unable to pick up on Hélène's devout wish, though it was perceptible after the death of Elie, and it is here that in these memories of my childhood and teenage years the presence of Toulouse in *The Red Scarf* takes on another meaning. Does it stand for, principally, the town where a man had to survive, childless and far from home: this was the illusion he was under, in any case, which had rapidly to be dispelled?

No, because Toulouse is equally a cipher for my mother's relationship to her own origins, a relationship that gave birth to her dream, a dream that had moved and dazzled my childhood, enough to say, as I do with Cavalcanti, that '*questo cor mi fu morto poi chè'n Tolosa fui*'; to believe that I left my heart

18 The poet is referring to *Du Mouvement et de l'immobilité de Douve* (1953) and *Hier régnant désert* (1958) respectively, both published by Mercure de France.

to go live with her in Toulouse, dead to other people, makes me anxious that I was for a long time, for too long a time, just a devotee before an image, and in no way a friend to a real being.

Which is so often the case, as it happens, among those of us concerned with poetry but who think it can be born of words, at the risk of a rapidly growing anxiety. I can note now that the lady revered by Cavalcanti in Toulouse was not someone he had met in the town, in fact she had her dwelling in the Daurade, the great church with the golden vaulting—she was a statue, with one hand upraised to the heavens, and in the other—the left, on the side of the heart, the body—holding a scroll. This contained the Gospels, undoubtedly, but for the poet passing by, who makes a halt here, it is troubling, it gives him pause, and he thinks of his own book, its relations to writing and to speech, and with that the concurrent temptation to expect from it much, indeed too much. What did he write, or what could he write? In a critical moment for Florentine poetry, Cavalcanti asked this question, and the answer was his work. The *dolce stil nuovo* requires writing to help with the suppression of the views, concerns and desires of any particular existence. It is pledged to the reality of a superior form that would emerge from words as the sole being possible for a human life in search of itself.

And that is indeed to place a book in relation to the heavens, like the statue in the Daurade. But is it really to love? No, it is already Mallarmé, devoted to his project of the Book, in which the mind is trapped, just as a ship gets blocked in the ice floe; it is the opposite of Baudelaire whose 'passer-by' did indeed have a 'statuesque leg'—possessed, that is, of a beauty to set one dreaming of the power of forms and of an Ideal raised above the world—but more importantly she had a gaze seeking through this world, with the fever of hope. An eye that makes contact with other eyes, and could indeed engender, in one whose gaze she met, a 'sudden rebirth'. The sky, that day, was just a lid of cloud, where the storm growled, pierced by lightning. But not before an eternity stands revealed, lit up for an instant by that flash.

VII

I think again of the end of *The Red Sands*, or, rather, of the end I invented for it when I came to write *The Arrière-pays*, some years after the poem of 1964. At that time I had not recovered the little book. In the end I found it at the Bibliothèque Nationale, in a basket of similar pamphlets; I made a photocopy, but refrained from reading it, but that is what I shall do now.

So how does *The Red Sands* end? Obsessed by the thought of Cepheis, the boy who discovered the 'Pearl of the Sands' goes back down into the underground city, now deserted by its inhabitants; and there, in the hall where they first met, he finds her; she is waiting for him. The fact that she is still there, now alone and in danger, is obvious proof that she loves him, and on seeing him she cries out, from the bottom of her heart, the 'You, you!' that expresses her recovery of hope. Cepheis is ready to offer the 'young man' the red scarf of a life here and now—she is prepared to renounce for the future everything that the past has accumulated within her, and which dissolved like a dream.

But the young man's response to this is to say the least ambiguous. He loves her too, he assures her, and says 'Stay with me', but adds, oddly, that if he has returned it is also in the hope of finding the 'parchment', the book in which that past is written down, and which he wants to help preserve. At this, Cepheis cries out 'Adieu!' and, so I read, 'she vanished like a shadow, and he did not try and follow her'. The young man returns to the explorers' camp, troubled, 'his head down', but resigned, and ready to travel back to France, and prepared to listen during the journey to his father's lengthy descriptions of the peoples of Siberia.

Léon Lambry must in fact have realized that he still needed to write fifteen pages or so to reach the required sixty-four pages. To do this he invents a very boring episode involving stolen baggage, but which actually prolongs the intuition of discord between appearance and being which had made him disengage Rome from the sands and give life to his young queen. The baggage in question in fact contains the objects that father and son took from the deserted city. What had been concerned with being, has thus become a question merely of having. And it is the son who seems more concerned about the safety of the crates even than the father . . . A sad conclusion. He did love Cepheis but he loved even more the dream that she enabled, of a different, more prestigious reality, of a more elevated level of being. An hour of spiritual slumber which he does nothing to try and inter-rupt with an awakening, even if it means abandoning the dreamt-of figures to their lives in the crates, destined for museums: this is the world of the image, not of presence, of science and art, not poetry.

That then is the authentic ending of *The Red Sands*. And having subsequently reread what I wrote about the story in my 1972 book, I am startled, first of all, at the extent to which I transformed it. It is almost as though, from the start I had dreamt it rather than read it, taking over the principal characters, inventing their dialogues, speaking for them in turn, giving them thoughts and acts that are not in the orig-inal text, and reacting to these acts as if they had really taken place. In fact I was concerned about these lapses of memory, and what the cause might be. I wondered, in my *Arrière-pays*, whether it is what we read that dreams us, making us toys of forces which are active in the sentences we read; and whether we should not 'awaken from some of them, better to under-stand life'. Life, and also the dialectics of writing, has the power to enchant but perhaps also to prepare, by means of auto-criticism, for a 'true life'.

VIII

Had I woken up from *The Red Sands*? In any event I believe I now understand the reason for the ending, which was cer-tainly not a resolution that I invented for it, to replace the theft of the crates and the lectures on the peoples of Siberia.

In my memory, trains now went zigzagging across the steppes of central Asia; there were halts that lasted for days on end in stations whose names were incomprehensible to the two French travellers; they saw nothing but hordes on the platforms, peasants climbing down and others climbing up into the coaches, sellers of station food, baskets and beasts everywhere, among the shouting men and the silent women.

And it was in one of those lost stations that one morning, the archaeologist's son, still emerging from sleep had seen, through his open window, in a shock that went beyond mere surprise, and with much emotion, Cepheis, his lost love, waiting, a little apart from the heaving crowd. His mind, mistaken! How could Cepheis possibly be there, in the palpable here and now, when she had disappeared back into another world and another century? Could he rejoin her? He jumped down from the train and ran, but it was already too late; she was walking now, passing behind the station buildings, and then he lost sight of her. He sought her for a long time, but in vain, in that other unknown town.

What could this imagining mean, inspired perhaps by my discovery of Nerval in the late 1930s, and the *Filles du feu*? I think I know now.[19]

First of all it turned Cepheis, divested of her Roman garb, into the girl who is present always and everywhere, who

19 Notably, Gerard de Nerval's dream narrative 'Aurélia' which contains the despairing cry, quoted in *The Arrière-pays* in relation to Cepheis: '*Une seconde fois perdue!*' ('Lost! For a Second Time!', p. 49)

figured on the horizon of a life both as a possibility of exchange and proof that an inaugural experience of the self, lived out at the dawn of words, can remain only as nostalgia, as its secret: this incited me to think about the fundamentals of being in the world. But above all it is the lunge towards her, that first pursuit of a being belonging to this world, not an image, and the desperate renunciation, meaning that hope was rekindled, which implied a revival—drawing it into the self, allowing me to understand at last—that instinctive but contradictory *élan* that sweeps the self, imprisoned as it fatally is in its dreams, towards real existence. We speak; we have words to analyse the world, and therefore to lose it, we dream of what we lose, and we make mirages of it in which beings are beautiful but can never be seized, yes, but at least at times, within those very words, arises the intuition that the past that seemed lost is still open. Can one not in fact speak with them, speak, rather than ferment dreams, open up to the needs of the day now begun, observe the effects of time which unceasingly obliges us to make decisions and choices? The young queen who vanished into the sands of the unconscious, the obscure side of the palm garden, here she is, on this station platform, involved with this world, with concerns and preoccupations. The other is not the forever lost. We are offered a second chance to recover it.

Grasping this idea of Cepheis as existent not elsewhere but here, even if refused once more, this time in any case I realized that being represents the second chance for the mind initially so constantly tempted by the dream. It is this second level, that is not anything intelligible, not a heaven, not a superior degree of simple reality but the leap into the unknown of existence here, now, which is presented by that station in Central Asia, the travellers going about their daily business, and the girl whose escape from the other side of the wall is once more a message from Cepheis to the sleeping encampment: interdiction and invitation. One can jump out on to the platform. And when I distorted *The Red Sands* it was only for one moment of vain lucidity during a return to France, burdened with the scrapings of mere dreams, only one effect, and sign, of the anxiety, if tacitly expressed, behind *The Red Scarf*, and which the present book of exegesis and anamnesis is trying to appease and explain. Lost a second time? Ah, and how frequent it is, that the other life whose eye we sought turns away through our own fault! The other can only accede to itself through us, it owes us only its being; nothing will come of it if we do not help it to owe us everything. But what perishes in the representation that we make of it can be reborn as presence. And no matter if sometimes it lasts only for an instant! Life is never anything more than a flash that is frozen, just enough to let us glimpse, as it perhaps intends, great sleeping countries ranged everywhere around us in the night.

Danaë, the Hyacinth Girl,
Balin, the Mask from New Guinea

I

Thus far have I come in my thoughts about the pages that were written, let me see, exactly fifty years ago. I believe that I have come to understand much concerning their intention, and the anxieties that I was a prey to at that moment in my life, without being entirely aware of them. But I have not forgotten that the briefest scrap of writing results from an interweaving of causes, many of which lie outside the conscious mind of the author. The reader, on the other hand, who perceives the thought from what lies on the outside, is able from this very fact to have access to other points of view, not the author's own, but equally legitimate. A critical reading can be truthful in a way that diverges from the writer's, from the poet's own project, and can even invite a collaborative analysis.

Rather than continuing to soliloquize, therefore, at this point it is probably better that I should take into consideration such an exchange of views, and its possible value, and even to try and contribute to myself by supplying, not the meanings I believe I can decipher in *The Red Scarf*, but some information regarding certain facts behind the text: the association of ideas that I had in mind when I wrote, and which are valuable because poetry is metonymic more even than it is metaphoric. For it is where his experience overflows, meaning that someone wanting to be a poet realizes that these are the directions to follow. What lies at the edges of his thought is the richest vein. It is useful therefore to consult the notebooks mentioned at the opening of my poem, useful to say more about what they say, and especially, perhaps, if these other works, or facts, extend in all directions beyond the idea I have retained of them.

This is the one I must develop, however, I cannot do otherwise. For example, and in first place, take the 'Danaë and the shower of gold', which is the very first allusion made in *The Red Scarf*. Why does the myth of Danaë have so much importance for me? Because the shower of gold it brings forth, luminous and dazzling, is what I expect from poetry. A shower of gold? That is summer rain, the kind that does not cover the sun, but amplifies and deepens it, imprinting it onto the foliage it passes through, the patches of light it projects on aroused and laughing young bodies. Being comes to us in that rain, it is offered, and it is up to us to make an eternal morning out of it, from among loved things.

The shower of gold, summer rain, thousands of fugitive lights, are also the thousands of words in the language freed finally from their conceptual weight, living to the full their desire to dissolve into the very grounds of unity that appears in them like the sun through the shower: it is language attaining to that immediacy which I have always held to as its great potential. Danaë is the pledge made by poetry, it is that which rises above and beyond individual poems like a sudden bright spell. And which does not, be it said in passing, recognize itself in that other myth, of Orpheus losing Eurydice. Fabled singer that he was, Orpheus knew only the surface of things, as in conceptual thought. Orpheus was not an artist. It was not in him to live as Rimbaud once did, '*étincelle d'or de la lumière* nature'.[20]

And what of the 'morning in the museum'? Not, certainly, Titian or Tintoretto: even though they were Venetian and colourists, they remained too in thrall to *disegno* to allow form to soften outwards into light. Titian almost turns the shower of gold into coinage to pay off the courtesan. Correggio would be more likely, with his great intuition, `ho had no hesitation in placing within the tower-prison a view of a wide bay that gives way onto a vast horizon at dawn which makes of the approaching god, the sky itself.

There exists one more Danaë in great art. The painting I had in mind when I wrote *The Red Scarf* is Rembrandt's famous canvas. I have never seen it 'at the museum', I have not been that fortunate, but the poet-painter's vision is itself a veritable morning, transforming a very ordinary room— bed, clothes folded over the backs of chairs, shoes—into a space fit for the transfigured arrival of a god. Rembrandt's

20 ' . . . flash of gold in *unmediated* light' (Rimbaud, *Une saison en enfer*, 1873).

Danaë is not a young captive but a woman of her time, who has seen life, as the saying goes, who goes into town, and comes home, who has a servant and a busy daily life. What does he mean by this? That the soul has its prison, and its hope, at every moment and in every place where the self is in relation to being. There is no clearer way of indicating that Danaë is poetry. No better example could be found for someone concerned with poetry, and who thinks about it in his notebooks.

II

A similar kind of analysis in another notebook revolves around a line by T. S. Eliot, 'The hyacinth girl' who appears, arms full of flowers, in *The Waste Land*.

I should say at the outset that I do not adhere to his idea of poetry in this great poem. I reproach Eliot for consenting too readily to the desolation he can evoke with such skill. His lines—in the waste land, by which he also means the country to the west, lands of the setting sun—are merely sterile existences, emptied of meaning, and even more of hope, which is of course a state that exists, and not only in the London fog, where the living are already dead, as in Mallarmé's poem 'Toast funèbre'. But why respond to what is in any case so evident, with self-derision? Is it not to give up on hope, which is the heart of life? An entire century has suffered from the 'hollow men', from the 'stuffed men', who prattle and stagger, as Eliot has them do, on the threshold of post-modernity.

There is, however, an oasis in this desert. There are some lines in which someone speaks, and someone answers, there is the beginning of an exchange. Eliot has just evoked the desperate end of *Tristan and Isolde*. But without transition, he writes:

'You gave me hyacinths first a year ago;
They called me the hyacinth girl.'
—Yet when we came back, late, from the hyacinth
    garden,
Your arms full, and your hair wet, I could not
Speak, and my eyes failed, I was neither
Living nor dead, and I knew nothing
Looking into the heart of light, the silence.
Oed'und leer das Meer

and suddenly it is like a bright spell as in this return from a garden on a summer evening a girl appears with flowers in her arms and her hair wet as if a wave had just washed over her. Sifted through the branches of the great trees one can feel close by, an intense light bathes the young woman and her companion in a play of rays and shadows and it matters little if her lover fails to find words to express his attachment to that moment in that place, he knows that speech would be its ultimate expression, in that it favours exchange. Eliot seems ready to comprehend what poetry attests.

But it is not simply because these lines are written under the sign of Danaë that I alluded to them in *The Red Scarf*, it is because they showed me how the summer rain can fail to illuminate language. With her heavy hyacinths, those androgynous flowers, and her long hair, the girl summoned by Eliot is based less on a real memory than on a figure in a dream. The diaeresis in 'hyacinth', so readily noticeable when the lines are spoken aloud—it is repeated twice—is one of those beautiful falterings in the form that, as with certain painters, betray the intrusion of subjectivity, that raiser-up of chimeras, into the perception of what is. In this 'hyacinth' there is the same suspicion of goitre, that thickness around the throat, found in the Italian beauties drawn by Dante Gabriel Rossetti, whose paintings have trouble concealing that they are images, and not life.

Eliot's 'hyacinth girl' does not have the 'red mournful lips' of Yeats's Maud Gonne, this latter being for the poet consciously torn between existence and dream. The former is the image that due to its very incompletion as image, its ignorance of the flesh-and-blood body, of lived time, of death, becomes detached from what is, leads us to mistake it, and lays it waste. And it convinces the author of *The Waste Land* that *Oed' und leer* is the sea separating Isolde from Tristan.

And if I evoked 'the hyacinth girl' in *The Red Scarf*, it is because I too am vulnerable to seduction by images, I experience them as a danger. Is the only way to refuse nothingness to imagine forgeries of being? Does beauty exist on the earth only to cover over the terrors of the abyss? Are we therefore, decidedly, the lands of the West, of the setting sun, where human exchange must wither away, being itself no more than factitious beauty or blind violence? In the narrative by Chrétien de Troyes, which Eliot had read, but not sufficiently pondered, the disaster has a cause; and Perceval is astonished, and in wonder, to see carried before him a spear dripping blood, and a golden vessel covered with precious stones: much strangeness, but also beauty, rich things that make him forget to ask—to whom is the Grail bearing food?

III

Perceval? It was when I came to deal with the nature of the image in the poem that I read the Arthurian cycle, which enabled me also to go some way to explaining the third allusion at the start of *The Red Scarf*. I have no doubt that the words in question, 'he heard an horn blow', 'knight of the two swords', were copied by me into a notebook; this would have been in London, in 1950, when I was there on a scholarship, and I discovered *Le Morte d'Arthur*, that immense compilation made by Thomas Malory in the fifteenth century, of all the Breton narratives, some of which would be unknown today without his mediation. This book is pure poetry, for pages on end, and the two phrases I quote in *The Red Scarf* must have struck me forcibly, to say the least.

I was reading the story of Sir Balin. After numerous adventures, Balin finds himself in the dark midst of a forest he does not know, when suddenly, from far off, comes the sound of a horn. The hunting horn is a voice, and it speaks to us of ourselves. Indifferent to the fate of the hunters, in solidarity with their prey, the horn laments and suffers; it requires of us to consider that in our own lives perhaps the Kill is near, perhaps it is too late already. Balin stops short, listens to the horn, understands what it is telling him. Does he turn back? No, he pushes on, without knowing where. He surrenders to a drive within him.

He is soon at the entrance to a castle, where a maiden welcomes him, and says the words I transcribed in *The Red Scarf*: 'knight of the two swords ye must have ado'. What that entails is not yet clear, but 'ado' is one of those fundamental words that come from the darkest depth of languages, it speaks of life and death; and in the mysterious castle it would seem that the new arrival who knows not what to expect will be confronted with life-changing situations.

Now, we know that up until then Balin has not stopped, throughout his adventures, from committing what Rimbaud, in *les Déserts de l'amour*, called 'sad, strange errors', sometimes with tragic consequences, errors that cause deaths, as if this well-intentioned and entirely generous knight were under a curse, as inexorable as it is incomprehensible. In particular, and above all, he had delivered the 'dolorous stroke'. That took place in a different castle, in the struggle against an invisible knight, during which Balin had substituted his unlucky sword for a spear which struck home against his strange adversary, upon which life everywhere in the world stopped· Balin was the cause of the arid land that Chrétien de Troyes associated with the destiny of Perceval.

'Ye must have ado!' The event will consist of an ordeal in which Balin must triumph; if not, he will die. And then, all of a sudden, there he is, up against a masked knight who barred him passage, in a deadly struggle, a fight to the death, executed with a strange inexorable violence, until both of them expire, covered with the same dreadful wounds. But in the final, agonizing moments, when they have fallen in a heap together, in the strange solitude of this place of combat, they remove their helmets, their faces appear, and they look at each other with stupefaction, and with grief, for the adversary so ferociously and blindly engaged in combat is none other than Balan, Balin's dearly beloved brother!

This is the struggle I wrote of in *The Red Scarf*, impulsively, and more than ten years after I had read Malory:

And the combat will go on unceasingly,
The two warriors have dismounted,
Seeking the throat with their swords,
Their blood flows into the grass, night falls.
Now they are on their knees, they stab each other,
Ah, my brother, but why, why?
They collapse against each other, on each other,
Pierced with the same metal,

and I now see clearly why I had to do this, at the moment in my narrative when the person representing me had arrived at a stranger's door, in Toulouse, and finding apparently, appearing brusquely in front of him, someone he doesn't know, as when I wrote it I did not yet know, or did not want to know.

I received a shock, reading that page of Malory, and I reacted in that way, because I recognized myself in Balin, 'the knight of the two swords'. In no way at all 'a passynge good man', as Balin was at the outset, but desiring to be so just as much as him; I had the sword that was gifted me by words to use in my fight for poetry as well as, like him, or so I feared, being rash enough to add to it the faulty blade made up of mirage and dream. Betrayed by the sword of dream, Balin delivered the 'dolorous stroke' that deprived being of life, and devastated all human exchange, devoted entirely now to 'enchantments', that today would probably be known as fantasies, and neuroses. And what of I, the dreamer, what had I done? What had I risked, or put at risk?

Is Balin myself? Must I acknowledge his fate, his blindness, in the crumbling wall and the bird of night at the end of *The Red Scarf*? I think now that I was so attached to him because I knew I was by no means the only one to start on that adventure yet again. All who dip their pen in the black ink of the most luminous reveries make the same mistakes as the knight of the two swords, and run the same risks, and it is as if the story whose French original is lost—which is no accident, incidentally, it transgressed the conventions—perfectly enacted the split which divides and devastates self-knowledge when it allows words to abdicate their task at the here and now of life, to imagine other worlds.

These three allusions, then, at the opening of my poem: they prove that the latter is as much a reflection about poetry itself, as it is an ingathering of my regrets and my anxieties. But there is also the notion that these two concerns are in fact one and the same.

IV

There is still one more allusion I need to explicate in *The Red Scarf*, and I can see that it will confirm the link between the two elements surrounding my idea of poetry.

This further recourse to metonymy is the final one in the poem, which may in itself mean something, but it differs from the other three in a way that certainly marks it out. The others are to be found in the 'first fragment', which was just the sketching out of an idea within the space of a piece of writing. And the second fragment starts in the same way, but suddenly it seems that this work is interrupted. For somebody appears, on to what becomes a stage. I have him say, 'The next day, he said to me', which shows that the 'idea for a story' had also been for words spoken out loud; furthermore, shortly after this witness adds, 'it was then that my friend became afraid', which suggests that the ideas and memories written into the text that went before do indeed belong to a person existing under the gaze of someone else; that he is perceived, and to be perceived, by this external viewpoint that sees things in his being that the subject does not himself see. This introduces a new sort of complexity to the original idea for a story.

> It is dark when he tells me all this.
> He leans forward to light the lamp.
> He straightens up with it between his hands,
> He holds it so close that the red of the lampshade
> Streams upon his chest,

states this other voice, and now the person who spoke about a red scarf and Toulouse is seen at his home. And it is at this exact moment in my story that the allusion to be explained occurs. 'Listen', says the man bent over his lamp, and then adds:

> Another memory returns,
> I am crossing a bridge,
> Holding something in a brownish bag,
> Where am I, in what town,
> The river flows swiftly, it seems to swell
> By the minute, is there
> Another bank on the far side? And what might be
> These shadows drawing near, so tightly
> Pressed one against the other, in the rain
> That is now falling? I open the bag,
> It contains a mask from New Guinea.

Like a crescent moon.
I just purchased it from an antiquarian,
But it too frightened me,
And I rushed to return it the next morning,

—none of which appears to have anything to do with the matter of *The Red Scarf.*

But it makes sense to me, the mystified author of this poem, because this time it is a memory from my conscious life, an account of an event that really did happen.

A mask from New Guinea! But first, Cambridge, Massachussetts, in 1963, barely a year before I wrote out *The Red Scarf.* Lucie and I were happy to be living once more—and for an entire semester this time—in this town so alive with knowledge and intelligence, all the more so as we had lodgings on one of the streets that gave on to Brattle Street, the heart, if not indeed the brain of the town. Brattle Street was on the old road that plunged straight towards Concord and Walden Pond, into the very heart of American history. Nowadays, just further along than the bookshops and delis on Harvard Square, one can see the Brattle Theater, with its basement bar, The Casablanca, then a convenient meeting point for friends. Close by this cinema-cum-museum, in our time there was a shop that sold objects and artworks from ancient or—as people used to say—primitive cultures, that belonged to Bernard Bernheimer.

Cambridge 1963: one of my happiest memories. Jorge Guillén, the poet in exile, was just around the corner, Pierre

Boulez was giving the Norton Lectures, Robert Lowell, Jack Sweeney, Robert Fitzgerald—translator of Greek tragedy, Homer and Virgil—were all teaching at Harvard, and we would meet these friends and others, at their place, or at ours, or at the Casablanca, or in the restaurants of Boston or Harvard Square. And on all sides, forming and widening, was that wave of lucid and enthusiastic young people— courageous too, they were preparing to head South to witness the black population enrolling on the electoral lists—that soon became the flower children during the period of the Vietnam War, of Bob Dylan and Joan Baez. Angela Davis, laughing and wild-haired, came to hear about Rimbaud in my poetry class, and about Hegel and Marx with Herbert Marcuse, in the class next door. In August, Martin Luther King proclaimed his Dream. At the same time, in addition to my courses at Brandeis University, I was translating Yeats, which was like quenching my thirst at the very source.

And nearby our house was this antique shop. It contained few 'fine pieces', as they are rather idly called, but a mixture of all sorts, often nothing very special, but all of it jumbled there together, a chaos that seemed to leave Bernard Bernheimer admirably unmoved. Why did we keep coming back to see this affable man, who became something of a friend, and who would stand up smiling and extend his hand, with just a single lamp on his desk to light up the shop, on those wintry late afternoons, when snow was in the air? We had good reasons for doing so.

V

The reasons were connected to our lives, that were then in movement again. I have spoken of the silences that had so affected, so disconcerted my childhood and my teenage years, and my companion, Lucie, had experienced the same. They sprang from our origins, that my father, and hers, were almost ashamed of, and never mentioned, while our mothers did so only to feed their own dreams. They had not entirely wiped from our thoughts and desires, the tree, the stream, the track, the stones, the places they could have named, but they obscured the ways in which our parents had lived with them their first years of life, listening to legends, observing little rituals, preparing for seasonal festivals. As for us, we were moderns. The trees no longer bent over us to offer their ripe fruits. The plum trees in the little orchard in Toirac could give me savour but not sense.

So what was left for us to do but, when the right time came, seek out the books that spoke to us of ancient societies: for example, the *Popol Vuh* from Guatemala, in Georges Raynaud's masterly translation, was a revelation, and as important to me as any poem. I badly needed these books. The study of societies that predated monotheism, or struggled with its early impact, provided an antidote to the evil that I felt had invaded poetry. I also went to hear Henri-Charles Puech speak about the Gnostics, whom I needed to be cured of, and I borrowed from a very cultured and learned friend books on the Prairie Indians. Was I transforming myself into an American-style historian of late period Egypt? It was all a chimera. I did not have the philological grounding, and researching it would have taken far too much of my time.

But I did stay close to the axe, or the ploughshare, that I found one day, all dented and rusted over, near a house in Provence; I was attracted to those bowls fashioned directly out of wood, peasant baskets, pottery with hand-painted flowers and foliage, which is why Lucie like me frequented Bernheimer's shop in Cambridge, who sold such vases and pots pell-mell, from all over the world, mandalas and calendars from India, moving samples of Coptic fabrics, African masks, but also—and this was an important, ongoing discovery—the wonderful baskets for all occasions—including for boiling water—woven by Indian women all over the United States. An elementary language, that in Europe would become Poussin's great horizons, freed from the 'Knight of Sorrow' who wanted to bar my passage to a simplified vision of life.

We purchased baskets, bolts of fabric, Indian almanacs, and we carried it all away in those 'brown bags' obtained at the supermarket; they took their place, first in Mason Street, then in Paris, our two hearths. But there were other kinds of objects at Bernheimer's, who also sold masks set in certain expressions, often of horror, the handiwork of societies terrified by typhoons and wild beasts, retrenched in a bare, minimal sense of existence, comforted by nothing outside of it. This time indeed nothingness overtook being. The horror of life as expressed by the Gnostic thinkers seemed justified by these masks. It was the dangerous retinue surrounding the sorrowing knight.

So was Bernheimer not merely the simple dispenser of things that helped one to live, but an ironist, a witness, more suffering than perverse, undoubtedly, of the double condition of being human? A thinking being who kept in the gloom of his basement the sprung trap in which, so often, life got snared by the earliest usages of language? But by the same token did he not offer his visitors a chance to realize this, and take cognizance of the mind's fragility? That, at least, is what I often pondered as I left his shop and crossed Brattle street, as darkness fell upon the snow.

VI

It is the memory of these pleasures, but also of these fears that appears when the lamp with the red shade throws so little light upon the man who speaks, who falls silent, who speaks again. 'I see myself crossing a bridge'? The Charles River does not flow between Brattle Street and Mason Street, but a river swells in me sometimes, the one evoked by Eliot in *The Waste Land*, when he sees the numberless crowd of the dead pressing to get to the other side. Are we then just our '*spectre futur*', as Mallarmé feared?[21]

21 '*Nous sommes la triste opacité de nos spectres futurs*' (We are the sad obscurity of our future ghosts) (Stéphane Mallarmé, 'Toast funèbre', *Le Tombeau de Théophile Gautier*, 1873).

Should our knowledge of the rain be restricted merely to the cold foggy mornings in great cities? Must the proofs of non-being triumph over the illusion of being? What is it we hold in our hands, clutched in a bag of 'brownish paper'?

'I open the bag', I find the 'mask from New Guinea'. And I did in fact purchase from Bernheimer, during one of those evening visits, on an impulse, an object that was in fact less a mask than a thin face fashioned of wood and jute, carved in profile with a strange laugh, a crescent moon reflecting the ray of a star, a malevolent star, I feel sure. This thing was absolutely one of the items usurped by non-being in the chaos of that shop. Admitted to Mason Street, and into our lives, it would have been an ill omen. Why did I ever want it? 'I rushed to return it' the next morning. A few years later we redeemed ourselves in the eyes of Bernheimer by finding something else.

VII

But the man who recalls in *The Red Scarf* the mask from New Guinea seems to have been more troubled by his purchase than reassured by its return the next morning, after the thing was seen in the cold light of day. And I note now that the memory came back to him at the moment when, thinking of the visitor who arrived from Toulouse, he admitted that the feeling this had later inspired, was not only fascination but also hostility. Entering as I do, at nightfall, into the space of my fiction which had been closed upon itself until then, lighting the lamp with the red shade, standing up with it in my hands, am I there to put into doubt, if not the meaning that the poem seeks to give to my life, then at least whether my deciphering is sufficient? Am I ready to acknowledge the undertow of my thought, which I should not deny but rather visit, and explore: the moment upstream of words in a life, the earliest drives being the ground laid over the fissures, the slippages, the occasional obscure rumblings on which we have to build our dwellings?

I note also—I note now—not what precedes, but rather what follows the interjection of speech that occurs in the text. There is an evocation of a train taken by the character who rushes to Toulouse. This train 'thunders between bare, greyish rock walls', above which thunders the storm of unknown and possibly unknowable forces, while birds like ghouls hurtle against the windows. In the coach, the traveller is jostled by shades, who lead him to understand, 'with laughter', that they know more about him than he does himself. Where he is going, he no longer knows, a prey to 'ancient terrors', 'sometimes almost crawling in the mud', passing thresholds in the inky night so he discovers the truth of what he 'thought to be the day'. In all likelihood, the long passage is the admission, in *The Red Scarf*, of the active presence of an unconscious force that has been repressed. The night goes, he goes, to Toulouse, and it matters that his memory is with him, scribbling down on his knee, 'squatting' right next to him, everything that is heard in this night of troubled sleep.

Yes, but I know that train very well, it's the one we used to take, my parents and I, in those far-off years when, at the start of summer, we would leave for Toirac, and I never quite knew if the world down there was the same as this one. We would zigzag past great stations with strange names, first Vierzon, then Chateauroux, and finally Capdenac, through lands I knew and saw nothing of, being aware only of the long tunnels that seemed to be the soul of them, the sound of the axles changing abruptly. There were halts at platforms where beings emerging out of nowhere rushed about under our windows that were sometimes misted over, and a clarion voice would override the others to announce 'Brive-la-Gaillarde', 'Limoges-la-Souterraine'. What was this 'gaillarde', this 'souterraine'? Beautiful young women, old and wicked fairies? I would press my forehead against the cold black window.

But finally through all this noise and darkness, I saw the day begin to break, revealing on the horizon a range of low mountains that seemed withdrawn into their own space and time, indifferent to our lives. Daybreak is without end. Movements start to stir low in the sky, sudden brilliant spells run along the earth, many a times the darkness obscures the light again, but when the latter triumphs, there remain dark patches, and narrow currents running between them still, in silence. The dawn, watched from a train, when one is a child, will remain vivid in the memory for the rest of one's existence. So it is that I think with emotion of a fire I glimpsed at the end of one of those journeys, a little away from the tracks, a fire of branches moving among stones, in the brambles. It had just been lit, since the red flames were only beginning to emerge from whirls of thick smoke. But who had started it? There was no one to be seen.

1964–2015

June–December 2015

Pierre Jean Jouve

As I correct the proofs of *The Red Scarf*, I note that in this recollection of how I came to poetry, I have not mentioned one body of work that nevertheless played a major role in the matter. Especially since, over the years, I have never stopped stressing how important it was for me.

Why does Jouve not figure in *The Red Scarf*? Because what I owe him is not on the same plane as the matter in hand, a work of memory and reflection focused on my relationship with my parents, whose lives influenced my own ideas about the nature of poetry: setting there my apprehension of finitude, and my conviction that the experience of life lived through time (*temps vécu*) alone can bring language alive. I had this thought within me, though it was scarcely conscious yet, when in a bookshop in Poitiers, sometime during my nineteenth year, I came across some books by a poet I didn't know, Pierre Jean Jouve. These books did not, therefore, play a role in the account I have just given. Jouve was important to me in a different way.

What then was the role that Jouve played, distinct from my own nascent consciousness of self, and yet assuredly essential to what it expected of me, hence the emotion that overwhelmed me on reading the first words, standing near the door in a bookshop I'd just happened to enter? I need to understand what happened to me at that moment, but in fact, it is not complicated. A year or two earlier I had discovered the Surrealists, and I adhered, or wanted to adhere to their values and ambitions, but instinctively I remained attached to words employed in a rhythmic pattern. Which is why, listening to Breton, and letting myself be seduced by that oratorical prose—Breton's poems are speeches too—I remained a reader of Valéry's poems, all the while starting to feel an unease which crystallized when I read *Matière celeste*.

I had been fascinated, ensnared, by 'Le Cimetière marin', by '*ce toit tranquille où marchent des colombes*'.[22] And now,

Incomparable terre verte douce et funèbre
De collines avec châteaux et ombres[23]

what a different relation to things, to situations and to calls to life, what a relief! These two openings to a poem contain a similar panoramic view, and both describe less-perceived realities than the horizon behind them, and they evoke in microcosm the world as these poets experience it: and how different and how much deeper goes Pierre Jean Jouve's way of apprehending what is, and what is possible, and to follow that, going beyond tropes and similes that thought conceives and decides is the truth!

22 'This tranquil roof, where the doves are walking' (Paul Valéry, 'Le Cimetière marin', 1922).

23 'Incomparable earth green tender and funereal / Hills with castles and shadows' (Pierre Jean Jouve, 'Matière céleste', 1937).

If the sails, seen more or less in the distance on the sea, remind Valéry of doves, it is because he limits his perception to what the intellect scoops out of the teeming mass of impressions taken at the first instant of consciousness. The comparison is constructed out of appearances—form, colour—and they only suggest themselves spontaneously to the mind, because the mind has reduced what doves and sails might be, as it does every other thing or event, to a network of preconceptualized ideas to which he identifies being in the world.

The prosody of 'Le Cimetière marin' confirms and reinforces the abstraction. No hiatus is allowed between the words of the poem, each one merging seamlessly into the one following, the final syllable of one elided into the first of the next: the mute 'e' is never allowed to warp the verbal skein; there is an almost faultless orchestrated continuo of full sounds which helps thought to put generalities of all kinds in place of time, chance, contradiction, death, the specific existence: what I call finitude. Immediacy persists, in this submission of reality to the mind, only in the pure sensation of the kind that satisfies the body at a moment it dreams of timelessness: the midday bathe in the sea.

It is true that a vestigial feeling for the finite does haunt what is actively sought here—a high noon of intelligibility— and in fact it is this unavowed anxiety that draws one to this great poem. The wind rises, we must try to live, exclaims the author suddenly, feeling that the breaking of a great wave will 'shatter' the tranquil surface, but at the same time this marks the end of the poem. Valéry refuses his own intuition—his own meaning, his own exigency—and is obliged to repress it in his words but also in his days, as in all his speculations and meditations carried out in the early hours in his *Cahiers*. Valéry may well mention tombs, but he neither manages nor seeks to look steadily upon death.

And suddenly there are these lines by Pierre Jean Jouve! They are so intensely the opposite of that attempt to reduce being to intelligibility. Here, all the mute 'e's are foregrounded, colliding against sounds that refuse any elision, and this deepens the line, tearing into what would have been conscious control, rhetoric, '*terre*', '*châteaux*' emerge as live presences as conceptual meanings are dispersed. The reality that intellect had dismantled came together once more, the gaze could uninterruptedly perceive the unity of all in all— the Alpine light in *Matière celeste*, glittering, intoxicating, at the heart of each mortal thing.

As for the woman 'with the black back', the one who 'was moving away', she who 'burst out laughing in the green valley'—these must be the traces of events or beings, whether real or imaginary, who must have left, put more clearly, their network of meanings on the text, but the meaning flowered underneath the words in such an allusive and enigmatic way, that it did not reduce language to its intention; instead it granted to the situations in human life, just by alluding to them, and by not obliging the reader to ponder the meaning of the case in hand, a plenitude without any obvious content, and so more mysterious still, the equivalent in what it promised, of those storied castles in the distance, on a 'funereal', but 'green', but 'incomparable', landscape of absolutes. These poems of Jouve made epiphanies out of words. Their potential, when they merely disappeared into meaning, meant they were turned in on themselves, stifled, forced into coherence: now they flowered, and intelligible discourse dissolved into poetry.

As far as I was concerned, I did not try and understand, in my first, liberating readings in Jouve, what he meant by— the stranger, I knew only the name—the 'ill-matched', the 'bad husband'. Without hesitation, I turned my eyes away from everything that did not attract me in those pages, the heavily sexual, the religious obsessions, of which there was a lot! The brevity of the allusions, and their obscurity when there was so much light to help deliver me from my own reveries, the fictions with their abstract meanings held in the verse, I delayed trying to 'understand'.

For a long time, indeed, I refrained from reading Jouve's narratives and novels; when I did, many years later, I did so hastily and distractedly, until the day when, commissioned to write a piece on the poet for the *Cahier de l'Herne*, I set myself the task of meeting him at moments of his life and in the intuitions and temptations of his thought. By that time I had got to know Jouve, and I felt affection for him, and I had no doubt that he merited attention on every level of a debate concerning poetry and dream, but I have to confess that when I became acquainted with what he dreamt of in that Hélène of the early verse, in his murderous Paulina, in his Catherine Crachat, not only was I lost in those tenebrous imaginings, but I felt no sympathy for them. I struggled to understand his meaning, but I could only conclude that this great poet had become trapped in one of the most noxious forms of Gnosticism, that which marks out sexuality as proof of the fallen nature of life, and of how the idea of original sin can haunt in a way that blocks the drive of words towards the world at hand, the simple—the very one to which poetry must attest.

This gnosis, or hermetic knowledge, is after all, so to speak, the infantile malady of poetry, and never afterwards entirely cured; and in that way Jouve, who suffered a bad dose of it, emerges only more truthful, and by a fatal contradiction, more truly a poet than most authors of his age, who were given up to moral or political utopias. Be that as it may, still I could not follow him into the world he had constructed, and in my approach to his work, I remained with the rent that *Matière celeste*—the title is a fine oxymoron—seemed to effect in the fabric of language. The outer details of an allusive narrative—the woman, the initial 'green', the laughter down the green valley—I considered to be the signifiers of that excess of being to be found in the depths of prosody, of which Baudelaire rightly said that in French it is as mysterious—in the strong sense of that word—as it is misapprehended.

Before reading Jouve, I had scarcely had any occasion to hear in verse a music as rugged or as moving, I knew nothing then of Rimbaud's last poems, or of '*Rêve intermittent d'une nuit triste*',[24] it was as though doors were suddenly flung open in the Racine of my childhood, with beyond it a whole new light in which I could stand, and progress . . . It is thanks to Jouve that I learnt to found my use of words on the powers of prosody, as the latter are employed beneath the collision of images. That I sought, in my *Anti-Platon*, still impregnated with Surrealism, to renew contact with the resonance of the great root words. Jouve rallied me to use the instrument that language can be. But this usage, its function, its true function, is to help the person writing to discover who he is, and to assume the particularity that is his only way through to the truth. And I could not, even a little, take that path, invest my words with the memory of presence, except by revisiting the situations, feelings, astonishments, thoughts that I had lived through in my own childhood, and that I have recounted in *The Red Scarf*. Very different matter, for sure, from the obsessions in *Sueur de sang* or in *Matière celeste*, even if, as I now realize, the name Hélène, which figures in the latter, must have exerted an unconscious attraction over me, which kept me close to Pierre Jean Jouve, even in those writings of his that divided us.

March 2016

---

24 'Intermittent dream of one sad night' (Marceline Desbordes-Valmore, *Poésies inédites*, 1860).

Two Stages

AND

Additional Notes

Two Stages

Still half asleep, there is this traveller, who slipped out of his hotel at daybreak and who ventures now into the old city of Turin, or of Genoa perhaps, where heavy stone facades go head to head, with their great worn boundary stones, massive recessed walls hiding beneath old iron bars their dusty panes. Who lives in these palaces? Is there any life in the turbid watery stretches of their silence? As if in answer there is a door ajar, I push it and I am under a long, low vault, at the end of which, the sun has risen so high, there is a bright courtyard, on the other side of a grille that is also ajar.

I pass through the grille, the courtyard is less deep and wide than the view of the building from the street might suggest, but it is beautiful, grippingly so, disturbing even, from the fact that all the window sills and lintels, and all the little sculptures that ornament them—but I can hardly make out the latter, because three sides of the courtyard are in shadow—form a single skein, whose heart lies at the centre of the elaborately worked cast-iron balustrade, on a balcony of the piano nobile of the principal dwelling, right in front of me. The salon balcony, definitely. The French windows with their little panes, that give on to it, are proof enough, and through them I can see the flickering of flames in all the chandeliers, still alight. Perhaps there has been dancing all night in these rooms, but now, what silence!

What silence? It is not the right word, for why did I not see all sorts of people, on that balcony, speaking to each other with great vivacity but quietly? It is still grey, on that side of the yard, it's true, and I can only make out the people, or the nobles, little by little, and with difficulty. Particoloured shadows. A red that flares up, suddenly, and then fades out. And faces, oh, those faces, but they dissolve so quickly I scarcely register them! Where has that giant draped in blue and green gone, who seemed, just now, to be terrorizing the whole right side of the stage, with that child on his shoulders, but also that big stick he holds up, and that laughter! In his place all I see are three or four little girls dressed in rags, each one holding—awkwardly, but they must be heavy—bundles of long branches whose tops are lost God knows where in the heavens, in the mists. And now someone is climbing over the balustrade, who is that? A boy, or another of these thin girls, legs floating above the void? Yes, a great tumult. I can hear cries, two or three very loud, and a piercing one, from far off, which terrifies, and freezes the blood.

Ah, memories, memories, what would you have with me, at this moment of my life? And why, all of a sudden, on this now brilliant stage, does the crowd of children and paupers divide? It is because a very beautiful young man and young woman, facing each other, advance on to the balcony. How they look at each other! And how they speak to each other, presently, how clear their voices sound around the courtyard that gives their voices back with a very gentle echo, albeit with a touch of irony here or there in the angles of three of the four facades. They are reciting a poem, most probably, or what in this world of ours we would call a poem, for their language is unfamiliar. What can they be saying to each other? Sometimes they make bold gestures, after which they remain, for an instant, frozen. Next, the boy has seized hold of the girl's arm, and he shakes her roughly, as though he were about to cry, and yes, he is crying, great sobs, his head laid against the shoulder that does not refuse him.

And I? Well, I wanted to speak as well, to say some words in that other language, and I try to do so, but no, I make just one sound, a simple sound that cannot escape me, that I stifled. But it is enough to draw the attention of the couple up there who can use the idiom that constitutes perhaps my own being, my own country. One that I used to speak, yes, I am sure of that now. And one that I can learn over again, I have no doubt. The man and the woman turn towards where the slight sound came from, astonished, searching the courtyard: which is now flagged, or becomes so under my eyes, with grass growing in the cracks.

But it climbs fast out of it, stands behind me and fixes, with astonishment or horror, how to tell, on a point of the fourth wall, the one under which I emerged from the vault. I turn around.

There is another balcony above the passageway, almost identical to the other, the same size, the same twisted black cast iron, spotted with rust. And the same sort of people are at the edge of the balustrade, judging from their voices, their laughter, and that cry, once more, of horror.

Is it the same play, being acted out on these two elevated stages, the same play in a mirror image, except a bit ahead on my side, and a bit behind on the other, in relation to what time present I know not, that must little by little come clear? But there is nothing behind me that resonates with the exuberance I witnessed just now on the other stage. There are even moments when I hear nothing at all, as if the balcony on my side were empty. This is not the case, however, because I can see the man and the woman quite clearly, who were speaking so animatedly, and who are now quiet, somewhat aged, and who are watching what is going on opposite them—watching, or at least endeavouring to do so. Their hands are almost clenched around the edge of the balcony. And the hand of one seeks a hand of the other, finds it and takes it and squeezes it hard, but without detaching it from the iron railing on which I see it open, turn over and relax, its fingers intertwining now with the other fingers. Yes, I see that, and it moves me or, let us say, I think I see that, for it is so dark.

They were anxious, and now they have hope. They spoke, and now they hold their breath. And I cannot remain here, for I do not exist it is they who exist. How, I do not know, but I go back through the passage, I am outside, meditatively I take a path that leads through tall grasses, and soon they are so tall that I can see only the sky and the first stars.

How hard it is to live! The little boy who had climbed over the balustrade his legs bare against the black iron, tries to walk alongside me, he has taken my hand, speaks to me. Who are you, he asks me, and I do not know how to answer. At this he bursts out laughing. And in my old language he starts to tell a confused story, about days spent by the water, when he and I used peaceably to go fishing with our rods. Oh, it was not about catching fish, he tells me, even if we had in those years little wicker baskets in which to put them. But the sun above us stood still. And we would remain on that riverbank of grass and sand, and wait for the evening that did not come.

2009

First Additional Note

AN AID TO UNDERSTANDING

I

Every traveller is given to dreaming, because what he sees is new for him, which disturbs his usual ways of seeing or understanding, and thus enables thoughts to return to him, those that had been repressed by a way of seeing, possibly since childhood. This can explain a disorder in the intellect, when the principles of logic no longer hold sway, for a time, over the apprehension of symbols: which is what happens in our dreams, when it is the unconscious that decides.

Every traveller? It is possibly above all applicable to anyone who wanders through Italy, because it is there, more frequently than in many other European countries, that one encounters the monuments and the images of a mode of thought that is essentially symbolic. The matter and the manner of this thought is thus revealed in Italy rather earlier than elsewhere, at least to certain visitors. And it requires of them, with some insistence, to revisit their desires, to understand that they are not necessarily just possessive in nature, having at their origin a need, and a nostalgia, for that plenitude within the immediate—to be brushed by that unity at certain instants of our lives—that the symbols speak of. Italy urges one to be lucid.

Have I, for my part, ever been lucid? Whether or no, it is certainly to that metaphysical space that I have felt drawn since my first day there by the successive civilizations of the Italian peninsula, the obscure primitive rites, the pessimistic wisdom of the Etruscans, the Roman order illuminated by Greek art, Christianity: systems that have never ceased to stir up the conflicts within me, the muddled aspirations, but which have strengthened, often enough, that hope which is at the heart of the poetic project. I had the kind of dream, backed up by an exegesis of the dream, of what Italy suggested. The traveller, only half-awake, was I, venturing out in the early morning into the labyrinth of signs in the *centro storico* of those towns, sometimes very small towns, where the vestiges of the past, images frequently concealed beneath other images, seem to hold out a promise, and for that very reason are rendered all the more enigmatic.

But why 'Turin perhaps or Genoa' in the present narrative? And above all, why did Genoa emerge, clearly identified as the background to these pages which continually surprised me, even as they took form under my eyes? To explain the presence of Genoa in my writings, I must first of all recall that the towns and provinces of Italy evolved through the centuries an idea of being and of life particular to each of them; but also that in the variety of these experiences and what they teach, one of the most important dimensions of the relationship of mind to world is often missing; and it teems with symbolic potential.

Florence, for instance, is a civilization entirely embedded in its Tuscan earth, the Arno offering no distraction, on the contrary—and the sea is far away. Siena, with its wide horizons leading towards Pienza and Montepulciano, is even more in the interior, it is the earth alone with itself; Umbria is the same. Rome has its seven hills—Ostia and its port form no part of its daily reality. As for Venice, is it really a city of the sea, no, it is much more devoted to its internal waters. A water that must be crossed and re-crossed ceaselessly, in the most ordinary moments of existence, water that is redolent with smell, colour, movement, whose glittering and ever-changing mists envelop and follow lives right through their front doors as much as the islands in the lagoon.

And Milan, Bologna, Turin itself! All things considered, the sea is but little present in the exchange of thought and image that went from town to town, which made the decisive contribution to the historic Italy that constitutes the Northern half of the peninsula; it was necessary to go down to Bari, or to Naples, to experience something else, and that is exactly what many travellers did, poets among them, including Goethe and Nerval, in search of something so vital to life that '*vedere Napoli, poi morire*' would be the phrase that encapsulated it the best, a metaphorical way of expressing the need for poetry.

But Genoa, then, Genoa, decisively part of Northern Italy, almost at the foot of the Alps, Genoa is a remarkable exception and fills a gap! A city, so solidly established in front of a sea right on the doorstep, and which arranges its quarters in stories, raked like the seats in a theatre, with the ocean for a stage, on which the dramas of sea and sky must have drawn responses from numberless spectators down the centuries!

Genoa has its own distinctive voice in the Italian polyphony, and it is quite natural to think of the great port when entering Italy, to come via Turin and and recall that it is there, to the right of the road that traditionally went from the countries of the North down to Florence or Rome. I am therefore not surprised that Genoa should have come into my mind when, settling down to write, I gave the unconscious free rein. The unconscious that does not forget what at Florence, Siena or Bologna the intellect would have us not recognize.

II

And I am even less surprised, when I know that the drama which at Genoa or in the other great ports of the world is played out next to the sea—this drama, if not indeed this tragedy—is one of the most fundamental granted to the human, to the speaking being, to experience.

And after all, what is the sight of the sun setting on the sea in the evening, if it is not life encountering death, yet with the knowledge that tomorrow the light will once more fill the sky, even though it will rise from another point in space, and not from this strange harbour where the vessel in flames is now engulfed? A death, but one that speaks of resurrection to those gathered on the bank, caught in the *contre-jour* for the painter tempted to paint the scene. Death, that required of these passers-by to turn from the sunset and reflect on what was already happening in the interior now covered in darkness, if not in themselves, in those depths to be fathomed. Death which incites us to look at the sea itself, where the sun has been drowned, as another road leading to us here: if one could only read the currents, and discover that they are not all running out, one of them already preparing on the flaming horizon a lighter passage that tomorrow morning will break upon the shore.

Moreover there exists, in the setting sun, and in the reveries it incites, the star, in the paradoxical fullness of its presence, and the sea, which is so deeply lit up, the natural symbol of the conjunction and the union of man and woman, enabling one to hope that there exists in life, by adhering to his own will, the wherewithal to escape the fascination with non-being. This is surely Rimbaud's thought, when in one of his poems, overwhelmed with hope, he writes:

> *Elle est retrouvée.*
> *Quoi?—L'éternité.*
> *C'est la mer allée*
> *Avec le soleil,*[1]

1 'It is recovered. / What?—Eternity. / It is the sea gone away / With the sun' (Rimbaud, 'L'Eternité', *Vers de 1872*).

the verb *aller avec* (to go with) has quite clearly a sexual connotation, and the sea under the rays of the sun can bring to the imagination, a primal scene—in the Freudian sense of the term—where a father and a mother had taken delight in one another, and in so doing given an affirmation of life that Rimbaud never received. It is also the wish, in Baudelaire, expressed in '*soleil du soir, ruisselant et superbe*', the great poem of reconciliation, between a mother and a father, placed at the exact centre of *Les Fleurs du mal*.[2] Among the currents that intersect between the transfigured horizon and the shore, there exists one that returns to the great strand where humanity lights its lamps in the evening. A lot of meaning can be derived, clearly, in the brilliance of the setting sun.

Yes, but in Genoa, this meaning is perceptible only at the price of an ambiguity that inflects upon what the evening sky manifests, but it can also help us understand it better. The ambiguity lies in the fact that in the windows of this city, facing due South, the sun in fact sets on the right edge of the picture if not indeed out of the frame altogether. In the theatre of Genoa, the flaming disk is not in the centre of the image, and not even visible from many angles of the audience, so the most striking event in the sky is not in fact the most frequently encountered in this corner of the world. What is more easily remarked upon, I imagine, with the passage of the seasons, is how high the sun is above the horizon, the shadows

2 ' . . . evening sun, sovereign, streaming' (Baudelaire, 'Je n'ai pas oublié, voisine de la ville').

it casts, in the middle of the day, whether they are shorter or longer, how far the light extends over the floor in rooms where sometimes it shines through shutters.

The fact that the major drama is not exactly represented on the stage does not actually diminish, in Genoa, its impact on the spectator; the reverse is true, because things perceived at unplanned moments—by chance, a boat going out to sea, or in a high window—do not vanish from the consciousness; instead they become imprinted, and enlarged in the prism of memory, the metaphysical anxiety will only be more awake and more alert, and more rapidly capable of true intuition. To the extent that whether the sun is higher or lower in the sky, according to the seasons, the pulsing of light, that some memory of evening can blur might render being in the world a more complex and dialectical thought in this great port than in other places. The day proposes that we should love life, in the here and now; the evening, of which we only ever see a half, speaks of death, of non-being, inciting us to create reveries, and to create myths that promise supernatural afterlives: and Genoa, that sits slantwise before the sunset, is thus the place where dreams are made and renounced, a feast of illusion but also of unexpected resolution, if not indeed decisive movements beyond the aporia that haunt the speaking being, destined by his thought to be brought up short against enigma.

In the artistic exchanges that took place in Italy down the centuries, I wonder did Genoa not suggest a different conception of life and death than Florence or Venice? A different relation to the desires, temptations, acceptances and refusals that ravage our Western societies?

III

It is, in any case, with this question in mind, that I can now return to 'Turin or Genoa perhaps', and try and grasp what is really at stake in my text written under its sign. Turin, and thence to Genoa—to take the other fork at the great crossroads—so I may evade, at least for a moment, the austere attraction of the Florentine intellect? To go to Genoa, for the intuition I feel it offers, that I need perhaps, at every level of my consciousness, so that I may set some order into my lasting dilemmas? A need that grows more urgent as life passes?

Now that I reread these pages, which were written rapidly and without apparent direction, I see at once that they possess a greater coherence than I had thought at the outset. More, it seems that the text is made up of images so tightly plaited into each other, that I can only believe they had evolved together, unbeknownst to me, in what is called the unconscious; and it is indeed the latter, literally and figuratively, that the opening words seem to denote, both in the description of a sleep that is prolonged—the light sleep of morning, into which consciousness has already filtered—and in the idea of a labyrinth made of old streets and a vast, closed palace, which has a narrow entrance, an invitation to enter, to seek, but also, as I would soon learn, to hear and to listen. As for the meaning with which I invest Genoa, and the attention given simultaneously to the memory of the setting sun and the light of dawn, I see that it is also understood by my traveller, because he did not linger to open his eyes on the glittering sea before his windows, but slipped away among the sparse rays and the black shadows of the streets, which know nothing of the maritime horizon. Our capacity for the symbolic, that comes alive when we go to sleep, must find some interest in this double vision of Genoa; does it desire to beat a path into the interior, that other cities would not offer?

The silent palazzo, without windows giving on to the street, or only with ones sealed shut, as if for ever, must assuredly represent the unconscious: and it even seems to want to designate, to show itself as such, as if it desired that in my text I take due account of the place it must take in the interrogation that begins. And I have also to understand that what I subsequently see, once I have entered—following a low, vaulted passage, then a grille, also ajar—are actions, and actors, which are aspects of who I am, and possibly have been for long years. Did they take form in my dream just before waking, because the scene presented then had been lit by the sunset of the evening before but also by the other light, of ports turned towards the south, that one sees grow and lessen with the seasons, which are also the seasons of a man's life? In any case, I need to bear in mind that within the palace courtyard, with three of its facades still in shadow, the action is played out on one balcony, and soon on another, directly opposite the first: as if one of the conditions of life in Genoa—looking out from a balcony—is applied equally to the people in the play, one group staring out to sea, certainly beyond walls, and the others, those opposite, only at themselves.

That the dream which makes up my narrative is caused by my preoccupation with Genoa, I am fairly inclined to believe. And what follows afterwards will not dissuade me, for I can see within this tissue of brief events and fugitive figures a guiding thread, that I can easily interpret, being my aspiration, my old desire, which chimes well with my idea of a 'Genovese' view of life: a view that would be more inclusive than that afforded by Florence, and perhaps more dialectical even than in Venice.

IV

Of what does this preoccupation, this desire, consist? There is a prose poem by Rimbaud, that I have always found especially intriguing, 'Royauté'.

'One fine morning', writes Rimbaud, 'one fine morning, amongst a very gentle people, a magnificent man and woman proclaimed in the public square: "My friends, I want her to be Queen!", "I want to be Queen!" She laughed and trembled. He spoke to the friends of revelation, of the end of an ordeal. They swooned against each other.'

And he goes on: 'And they were indeed kings for a whole morning, and carmine banners were raised above the houses, and for the whole afternoon they processed along by the palm gardens.' The morning, the afternoon, but—and this is what strikes me—not the evening, the hour when Rimbaud, who was so spontaneously metaphysical, would have been obliged to add in the fires of sunset. Not the evening, and therefore, in this idea of 'royalty', there remains an open question, in which the pellucid light of morning and the already heavier light of the afternoon seem opposed to the spectacle in the evening sky, that brazier of visions so prodigal with promises that each one, is to be feared, is a mirage.

In 'Royauté', Rimbaud presents the question of the image: the image, which can transfigure life, with its figures that admit the fact of death, on their horizon—only to wipe it out by replacing it with worlds whose beauty, autonomy, panache, can exist manifestly only in dream.

It is because the man and the woman of his poem did not go—or not yet—towards the palm garden in the evening where he can speak on their behalf of 'the end of an ordeal' on that 'fine morning' which then offers them a destiny as kings and queens in the simplicity of life lived here, bare life, innocently sensual. 'Royauté' is Rimbaud's attempt to free himself from the 'cult of images', with its ceaseless illusions, which had been Baudelaire's passion, one which he did constrain—Baudelaire, poet of the setting sun, seen on 'evenings on the balcony, veiled in pink vapours'.

It is thus the expression of a hope; but in the hollow of the text, in its unconscious, so to speak, it does not disguise from itself a singularly dangerous temptation, one that would reinitiate the time of ordeal: so, a doubleness in the thought that I recognize easily as my own anxiety. I am strongly drawn to 'Royauté'. I understand the 'magnificent' man and woman, both as the highest possible form of the human, and the risk that they will be shipwrecked in the myths of the evening which will always belong to unreality, despite their beautiful reds gleaming across the palm garden. The poem also enables me to identify two personages at the centre of my narrative, a 'very beautiful' young man and young woman, 'who move out on to the balcony, turned towards each other'. 'How they look at each other!' I wrote, 'How they speak to each other!' Their speech is even what 'in this world we would call a poem'. Manifestly what is revived in this imagining is Rimbaud's dream of a humanity freed of its 'ancient enslavements', as he says elsewhere. The dream of the desire for being is deeper in each one of us than that of owning, of simply possessing.

But I have to remark also that I do not let the dream run its course, for the boy takes issue with the girl, he almost strikes her, but not out of violence or hostility, more out of sadness and distress: for now 'he is crying, great sobs, his head laid against the shoulder that does not refuse him'. Does that shoulder represent compassion, or 'charity', to use another of Rimbaud's words? No, it is scarcely more than expectation, and astonishment, for she is herself sad. The young woman has grasped her companion's unhappiness, and possibly understands the contradiction that torments him, but she does not have the words that would relieve him of this. So it is not the optimism of the morning hours of 'Royauté' that predominate for now, in my narrative, nor the temptation to dream before the 'golden galleons' of the sunset, but rather a thought about what can be said of life, life with its dreams which one soon discovers to be chimeras, and also its violence, and those precarious instants of peace, and the kind of love, difficult and yet deep, that can flower on that strand. Life, where one must learn to expect nothing from myths, but equally never to say that all trials end, 'one fine morning', once and for all. Life in which somebody's words may be what we call poems, but since poems are scarcely more than the effect and the reflection of a poet's contradictions, they will almost never entail a lasting attainment of that sovereign reality that poetry can glimpse.

Life, on the balcony, life and not dream, unless it be that nocturnal language, knowing and lucid, for which, it is true, we use the same word.

V

Life. And in consequence my own, in one way or another? Yes, and concerning the unfamiliar language, which awakes 'very tender echoes', I note that, projecting myself into the dream, I relate my desire to speak it, especially when the man sobs, but I realize that I cannot. I am tempted to do so, even knowing that it's impossible; but I would emit just one sound even though I note that it cannot escape my mouth, as if that stifled language was as much a part of my body as my mind. Clearly I am eager to participate in the scene on the balcony, in spite of the strangeness of the situation and the characters.

Why and how is it that I had no expectation to get involved, and what is the desire that I see is 'stifled'? To be struck dumb like this, suddenly and bafflingly, inevitably makes me think of those other times in dreams when a similar thing happens, something remains unsaid, an act the dreamer should have accomplished. Dream narratives abound in such clues, and they find their way into the most serious literature, the kind that approaches the concerns of poetry: it is the silence of Perceval, when he sees the cortège of the Grail pass before him in a dreamlike fashion, or it is Lancelot's stupor before the same Grail, that appears to him in his sleep.

The seizure of the will, which a sleeper experiences, recurs frequently in what one remembers of one's night-time dreams, where so much else gets lost, that I am tempted to think that it carries meaning, and in a manner that goes far beyond its specific occurrences.

To put this more clearly, I have always believed, since I first read the Arthurian legends, that the muteness of the sleeper conveys the incapacity of diurnal speech—submitted to conceptual structures and destined by this to analytical judgements—to pene-trate the mass of images or symbols that constitute as such dream activity. One can try and unpack the tissue, which is the work of the psychoanalyst, but one will not encounter, or one won't know how to encounter, interlocutors, and so at certain critical moments of action in the dream one will be beaten back, in anguish, onto the solitude of the self, that gives the illusion of being awake.

With this case in hand, however, I cannot accept the generality of this hypothesis, because a memory comes back to me, and a very personal one. I recall suddenly that my parents—who were still youthful when I was little—often spoke together in a language I did not know: this was the *patois*, as it was called, of their own childhoods. They did not teach me the patois, considering it merely a village dialect, spoken 'back home', whereas I was better off speaking the French of the purest type, that was to be found, it was said, in the town where they were exiled, and also my own birthplace. But I also know that in proportion to the distance put between it and I, which was almost a prohibition, that language, which was a variant of Occitan, very early on interested and even fascinated me, for two reasons that seem to complement each other.

For one thing, it gave me quick access to the dream of a country different to the town we lived in during those years, in many ways unwelcoming, which gave rise to incomprehensible situations: a world full of riddles that tended to stifle life. Faced with that reality, whose syntactic or lexical categories were structured strongly by the *langue d'oil* that we spoke, the patois made me desire a different one, that would convey meaning, and with it a warmth where one might live: the real becoming reality itself, the earth, an all-enveloping, maternal place. A dialectical process, whereby what was considered by the parents to be a drawback, viewed socially, now seemed to be a bonus, a surplus from the point of view of being. An idea of depth both straightforward and mysterious, where the society in question could only offer instances of abstract and dismally selective knowledge. An intuition of the world as substantial materiality, an emergence of unity. Was it, too, an illusion, a mirage—that language, that speech, forbidden and attractive in equal measure? Yes, I did come to grasp that one day, and how it carried within it all the perils of that metaphysical *imaginaire* that never refrains from conceiving ways of being in the world superior to those we know.

On the other hand, my parents also used the patois when they did not want their child to understand them, and they spoke quickly, using words in a way which had none of that seductive power, so clearly were they used to discussing the dreary anxieties of everyday life. And too often they were spoken with irritation, and even anger, in arguments and rows that would frighten the child listening. But it was precisely during these confrontations that he wanted most badly to speak the patois, so he could effect a reconciliation between mother and father, for his whole being depended upon their getting along.

These thoughts and memories come back to me. They do so with a force, a vehemence which leaves me in no doubt that they were already there, latently, when I wrote the narrative, but without consciously realizing it. And what can I conclude other than that the young man and the young woman of Rimbaud's poem only take on meaning in relation with my parents as they were during those years: bearing the trace of all their conflicts, their reconciliations, and invested, I am sure of it, with the desire that my own parents felt at that time: to surmount their current condition, of poverty and exile, full of frustration and unhappiness, and recover happiness and liberty in their exchanges, the good that Rimbaud evokes in 'Royauté'. My parents are there, in the penumbra of the grand *cortile* at daybreak. I relive, in front of that balcony, my lost desire, and my grief on realizing that my wish would remain unrealized. I know what the words are, that I was unable to utter.

VI

And now I begin to understand several other things. First of all, the very personal reason that is behind this balcony whose presence I have so far explained in terms of Genoa and its dramatic horizon. But if the young man and the young woman are in the image of my parents, what then is the balustrade, in front of the rooms that I can see are still lamp-lit as the dawn breaks?

I surmised at first that this was the scene of a wedding ball, a rich and joyful celebration, as if I regretted that my parents had not enjoyed such a thing when they married in the village. But no sooner have I thought that than another image takes its place; it is another sort of iron railing, the edge of the folding bed they used each night, once the dining table had been pushed back, and also used for homework. This is where my parents slept, and in my very early years I had my own bed, also made out of iron, with bars, next to theirs.

Earliest memories, so buried under later ones, that one recovers them only in fragments! But behind them is an entire horizon, of low hills and storm light. Reading Freud and his disciples and commentators, I have always felt that what he calls 'the primal scene' was not entirely understood either by him or them as it might have been, its full meaning only liable to understanding if considered on what I shall call the ontological plane, because the categories and issues are nothing less than the feeling of existing or not existing, the wish to be, or the acceptance not to be.

What is at the heart of this scene but a situation, an action that the child has no means of understanding, even though he feels directly affected by them? What he sees is an enigma, and what he feels also has the character of something that does not signify. Now, what happens when a meaning, whatever it may be, collapses, and when non-meaning appears to be substituted for it as the new reality, which becomes an obscurity, and thereby a darkness? Anguish can so submerge the observer, and the latter can experience the temptation to renounce trying to find his place in a world become impenetrable. The observer, as a result, is either doomed to a future made up of cynical thoughts, or else to a nascent desire to stop living.

But what he sees is not absolutely incomprehensible, he can sense there is acquiescence in these struggles, and tenderness in this violence, something like the echoes of pleasure, and so it is that, mingled with this state of non-meaning and of non-being, something else equally essential, which incites the observer not to fall into a fascination with non-being: in other words, to recover from this experience of the world into which nothingness has filtered, a thought about being, and the desire to believe in its possibility. The primal scene, or this example of the primal scene, proposes a choice between nothingness and being, and the moment of decision that enables the observer to meet the challenge of what frightens him, and to take control of his future.

There is a discouragement, or, also and already, a hope. And that choice is intimately associated with what one knows to be a possible existence, in as much as the exchange witnessed is formed against a background of rows and heated discussions the pair experience in their daily life, perhaps even a few moments before the unexpected dénouement in the darkened room. The strange and the misunderstood emerge now in relation to the continuity of daily existence; and instantly it is the latter, it is yesterday, tomorrow, the house, the world outside, which seem in imminent danger of collapse, all at once, or else they will go on, but in a different light.

The house with its cluttered little rooms, the sky that comes with the noise of distant trains, growing and fading away in the nearby suburb, the slender tree in the garden—and now, all my childhood memories that come flooding back at the mention of the iron cot; I have to conclude that, if the matter of the primal scene has especially preoccupied me in my reading of Freud, because I want to understand it better, and to gather it in as an origin in the reconquest of meaning, it is because it exists within me too, as an experience that mattered. My parents probably spoke in patois together, in those reaches of the night.

In me, yes, for as my narrative tells me, I wanted to speak, but without emitting anything more than a 'simple sound', but it was 'enough to draw the attention of the two up there, who are speaking in the idiom which is perhaps the fabric of my being'. ' The man and the woman turn towards the faint sound, astonished, seeking its source in the courtyard'; in what 'has become under my eyes' a flagged courtyard, as the text revises it on the instant. I am persuaded that this courtyard displaces a child's cot, situated below the adults' bed, 'up there'.

The adults, alerted, worried, what else do they do, this being so, than revert to their current life, with all its difficulties, and things touching upon their near immediate prospects? They turn toward what they once were, what they have now become, and to what they could be. I see clearly that this instant is a turning point in my own story too, just as it is also what struck me most when I wrote out that page without dreaming of avoiding anything. For the two balconies had in fact been my original idea. It began abruptly in a palace courtyard in Turin where, on turning around I saw the same long cast-ironwork balcony as that on the main facade. Following on from which, I wanted to speak about the two balconies, and to write about them, but for many years I had set nothing down, not having the slightest idea how to proceed.

VII

Let me now address, with an eye to understanding better, this sudden turning point in the story, the dramatic moment on that stage. The man and woman that I imagine, have been surprised by a sound that seems to be a stifled word, and they crane over to see where they fear it might have come from. But then they raise their eyes, and they are astonished and frightened by what they see.

On another balcony, at the same level as their own, and exactly alike, there are men and women, the sound of voices, laughter—and then, once again, a cry of horror—and they see readily that it is the same action going on where they are themselves, and including them, with the same secondary roles or more significant ones, and the same fundamental obscurity concerning the meaning of any and all of it: the only difference, at least to start with, is that over 'on my side'—behind me, that is—the play that is going on is a little bit ahead of what is going on opposite, on the first balcony. On the first stage then, the present, and on the other, the future? Undoubtedly, yes, because now behind me, the action continues, but more slowly, almost silently at times, while the man and the woman seen just before, are 'a little older now', watching what is going on, and what is there revealed, and they are visibly moved. They seek each other with their hands, make contact with the iron balustrade where they are leaning, signs of their solidarity in this moment of appraisal, and of shared affection. And this is moving to me, as I wrote, even if I still doubt somewhat what I am seeing.

They are anxious, but their gesture shows also that they have hope. Is it not as though, their moment of union over, their brief anxiety forgotten or possibly repressed, they had fallen asleep next to each other and were now listening to their dreams that merged their common destiny into a shared slumber? And that in turn reminds me of some pages I wrote, years ago now, on the boat of the two sleeps, 'that breathe close to each other'. In that poem, 'the two who sleep there have no face', there is nothing but their two naked bodies in the dawn light.[3] And the current is swift that carries the silent boat towards the distant sound of an estuary. And there is a

3 Yves Bonnefoy, 'La Barque aux deux sommeils' in *Ce qui fut sans lumière* (Paris: Mercure de France, 1987), pp. 98–102.

child in the bows of the boat, who feels compassion for these sleepers; who leans over that 'impoverished earth'.

The primal scene! It is my belief that one can understand nothing, or say nothing about it, unless one takes into consideration the aftermath of the initial astonishment felt by the observer, which substitutes for the terrified and devastating surprise he cannot decipher a wider view of the two beings involved, concerning their environment, and their existence generally at other times: on their life which is itself a mystery, with its impenetrable aspects, but also with its lights in the distance, between pillars of smoke, beyond the palm gardens. Life, which must teach that here, is perhaps a palm seed to be placed in the earth of one's being, a soil that will be fruitful if the first vision of the couple now sleeping can move beyond the merely outward apprehension, beyond the initial surprise and fear. I reread that poem, twenty years old now, included in the collection *Ce qui fut sans lumière*. There is a lot of desire in this poem, but also a good deal of hope. The child lights a fire in the bows of the boat, the river flows towards the sea, but it is clear water, with pebbles shining in its bed.

But how is it possible to move, as I consider it imperative to do, from dark night into the light? Here I need now to consult once more these pages rescued from my night, still soaked in my unconscious thought: and this time I am obliged to remark on its apparent pessimism.

For example, on the second balcony, which links the past and the future, the cry of horror that I heard on the first—the 'piercing' cry, that is frightening—rang out again this time, and will not, clearly, be effaced; what can it represent if not an act of violence, a rape even, against this festive background, full of laughter? Before the sexual act, which surprises the little child, and that astonishes him, was there perhaps some violence, some constraint, that ever after troubled the relations between the two partners, marked by haste and awkwardness, a strangeness that only adds to the astonishment of the observer? Disturbing also, is the agitation that reigned on the balcony before the young man and the young woman come forward, equivocal giants, among the children doing baffling things, the skinny little girls: the tumult of an unconscious one has been unable to set in order. More disturbing still, at least at first sight, is the way the two scenes disappear.

VIII

Indeed: 'I cannot remain here', decides the character who uses the 'I' pronoun in what I write; and I see him leaving the palace courtyard, returning under the porch between dream life and waking life—that other dream—leaving the protagonists of that night-time drama to live their own life, which is not his. He seems to lose interest in it all, he returns to himself. And what does he find, when he sets foot again in his ordinary existence? Not, to be sure, the Genovese street he had left for the double play, but a country track, where a little boy is with him, who takes his hand, one of the boys he had noticed on the balcony because he leapt over the balustrade, as if to escape from the dreamer's unconscious.

I know this child well, I have already encountered him, the one who 'wants to return', in several of my texts; and I can recognize him, and have done for a long while, he is me, but not as the infant who slept next to his parents: rather, he is a child of seven or eight, maybe ten, who asked questions about the patois, about words, and who started to get interested in poetry. He was also the owner of a ridiculous fishing rod, because from the grassy banks of the Loire, or the rockier ones of the Lot, he never caught a fish, and what is more, as I well know, he never really sought to.

And the pages I have written tell me more about this double, one in particular, in my central book, in which he appears in a tree, holding a cup in which burns a fire, but as the boat slips away, the boat in which, in the other poem, I saw a child, still a child, the same, nursing a fire on the prow.[4] Obviously this little boy has something he wants to tell me. And he does. 'Who are you?' I say. And he, laughingly: 'Who are you? Since you do not know how to blow out the flame?' One of those questions like a riddle, the kind encountered at thresholds, and which have to be answered if you want to

4 The poet is referring to his collection *Ce qui fut sans lumière*, in particular, to the poem 'L'Agitation du rêve', p. 83.

proceed further. The child added, 'Look, I blow out the world'. And then, what an oxymoron: 'it will be night, I will no longer see you, do you want only light?'

I have endlessly pondered the meaning of these lines, and I cannot give an answer, or even articulate the merest sound, because of some spell that has enthralled me 'further back than childhood', as I'd written then. I have wondered, not without anxiety, at what was suggested to me, with sympathy but astonishment; and what was the meaning of that sad sleep that had possessed all other existence around me, with revealed on the naked shoulders of the sleepers the red branded mark of slavery. And yet it was dawn, still dawn, though perhaps eternally submerged in mist. What does this poem mean, written at a moment in my life that had been, like no other before it, one in which I experienced everything at the same time while recognizing the illusory, the nothingness? What was it seeking to tell me?

What was it seeking? I think that I can, now, supply at least the beginning of an answer to that question; or, to put it better, I can begin to see more clearly the path I followed through those years.

I return now to the syncope in speech that my narrative of the two stages recounts. It was a syncope that had not been a repression, for the child at that age had nothing to say about a relationship between his parents that he could in no way interpret, but it was much more dangerously perhaps a collapse at the very heart of language: not to understand, on a level so obviously fundamental, turning all words, thoughts, images or beliefs into so many useless tools, empty envelopes, abandoned confidences. What was lived through, in that instant, was less a hindrance in speech than a radical 'muting'—*amuïssement*[5]—of any reason to speak. What was to be feared, was that any words, later, would be literally discouraged, stripped of their capacity to bear meaning.

This 'elision' or 'muting' is so frequent as well! Life presents numerous situations that a child on the threshold of thought cannot decipher, and now there are no myths able to coddle him with reassuring explanations; and empty speech, the type that is the rule in daily life, without any ambition for real understanding or exchange, is spreading now throughout society, and causing, among other perils, the over-development of conceptual thought. What was discouraging, was to believe that words have no credible leverage on unknown aspects of those nearest to us, without the strength to shed light on the needs or give help to share the desires: so that in this lack of understanding of life, the concept, less likely to treat of what is not measurable, is given free rein to explore the world from the exterior. The concept encourages the sciences that speak of matter, occulting as they do lived time with moments of unhappiness, anxiety or

5 Bonnefoy uses, by analogy, the word *amuïssement*, a technical term in phonology that designates the 'elision' of vowels or 'muting' of consonants, as language evolves; for example the disappearance in French of the original *s* in 'hôpital' or 'fenêtre', or in English the *k* sound in 'knife'.

joy. The gaze is turned upon the exterior, and that also disables understanding of dreams and their symbols.

IX

Had I been at risk of sinking in that way? I fear so, but I note that during this imminent danger I was helped, paradoxically, by the very language that would soon cause me suffering because I could not form sentences: the patois spoken by my parents, heard in their moments of stress; but also at other, more intimate moments, when the words used would be suddenly soft, and caressing, after the violent intonations that had frightened me earlier.

Whence came this help, and the decisive role played by unfamiliar words? Because an unknown language, for someone just at the threshold of their own, is a different sound, a sound that has no place in what he knows, a sound which obliges one to pay attention to the sound of a word, of its existence, yes, but also of the fact of its existence, as impenetrable as a star in outer space, or a stone on the path. Now, if one perceives of sound like this, upstream of all meaning, it can be the spade that breaks up the hardened ground of language, the lever that can upend worlds.

Let me explain. A word is a combination of a meaning and a sound. Normally, in verbal exchanges we pay attention only to the meaning, and we only register the sounds as differing phonemes, paying no attention to the sound as such. But the moment one appreciates how it overflows meaning, the moment one lets oneself be fascinated by, so to speak, the sound-in-itself, what an effect it has on our use of speech! One feels that the sound has a being, just as the sky, the earth, the universe itself; one perceives something in this being that cannot be broken down, and concepts—whose function is to treat events or things by aspects, that is from the outside—that can no longer claim, with this background now made visible, that they can exhaust any given matter: they are of the surface. Thereupon, for some of us, a change has been wrought, a discourse has been disturbed, and they seem to be mere superficial elements, if not indeed lies. But since words have always been there, vaster and more resonant, and deeper because they have sound, than the notions that leech off them, they feel that language is capable of a different type of utterance; and that a usage of words yet unknown but still accessible will enable the being that one is, a stranger to oneself, in exile, to recover one's place in the unity that emerges from out of this sound.

Such was my situation, my experience, my luck. A word in patois was not a sound I could attach to any meaning whatsoever. And hearing it must have given me a very great hope. Going down to the same level in my own language I dreamt of a relation between its familiar words that would repair the damage done by them in their daily usage, which would shake up their pernicious fixity, and that would spread about what is shareable: for it is a fact that the rhythms and assonances let the sound-in-itself emerge even in common

French phrases; every song is proof of this, and however humbly, it maintains the emergence of the One that afterwards we have merely to amplify in order to undo, it is to be hoped, the knots and the fixities of present existence.

A new type of speech, that can remove, relativize and strip out a part at least of their prestige, the notions, representations and values that are existentially without substance, those that divide the self, that set the body against the mind, imposing the wretched desire to have, to possess, at the cost of being, and cleaving first and foremost man from woman. A speech that would render the child's astonishment impossible, but also all the misunderstandings, conflicts and fears that had frightened him in others in those moments of surprise. A speech, a poetry, to scatter the enigmas just as the Knights of the Grail undid the spells that paralysed and laid waste to the land, rife with the kind of magic that proliferates when grounded meaning has been lost. I dreamt of this, albeit confusedly, and was lucky enough to start to dream like this, forming this kind of project.

Another fact, and another piece of good luck, enabled me to strengthen my dream in the years that followed. This was the absence, in the education I received, of religious instruction, works of art and lessons in morality. No one was there to try and turn me into a Catholic, or a Protestant, or even an atheist; no one urged me to admire Michelangelo or Shakespeare or Beethoven or Pascal, not even, apart from the history text books, to give me examples of how to live in society. In any case, I never had to submit, at least directly, to the redoubtable authority of any of these systems that reduce all of poetry in Europe to their own readings, which is yet another form of conceptual alienation. When one is at the receiving end of no particular tradition, it is easier to imagine oneself as the spokesman for humanity at its simplest, as poetry would wish.

Luck, in any case, is an impulse, whether or not illusory, that comes down from those far-off years; and I now see clearly it is this dream that I subsequently engaged, whether by directly working in words in my poems, or by the repeated affirmation, backed up by thought, of the validity of turning sound against concepts. This usage, the attention paid to symbols, to figures, to images that cannot be reduced to any conceptually formulated thought, has never ceased to fascinate and preoccupy me, creating in me the desire to listen to the various voices of the unconscious, heard most clearly at night, of understanding through symbols, to decipher what it is that that seeks to return to life, and which does, in certain poets, regenerating thereby something that in itself is quite other to their project, artistic production.

A programme, when all is said and done, as much as a task, with instruments to clear the ways and if possible to spare me from erring or giving up. But at certain moments during my undertaking, this child, standing in the cosmic tree, has appeared with a fire in his hands. What does he want of me? I am obliged, now, to understand.

X

First of all, he is contemporaneous with the astonishment that I embodied, when still without any conscious grasp of the project I have just described, and that one can easily criticize as being merely utopian. And he expresses the doubt I have never ceased to feel, if not concerning the validity, then at least of my capacity to do anything more than dislodge anything other than ideas and representations without leverage on the social and human reality that the centuries have forged. A world, that writing produces, mine like any other, but it may well be a world that is as much if not even more of a chimera than the speculative systems through which humanity has always debated. And rather than proceeding any further into the work, which is perpetually opening under our feet as subjectivity fraught with fantasies, why not just decide that what language produces will never be, at its very root, anything but some illusion or other? The hope remaining nevertheless—astonishing contradiction though it be—of contact with a unity that is divined, beyond all snares, like an undefeated presence, indifferent to our own ends here, but a light like the light behind the eyelids when pressed against by one's fingers.

'Look, how I blow—I put out—the world,' says the voice that was stifled within us. Look, there will be nothing left to us but light. How well I understand that suggestion! How well I understand that in the presence of worlds produced by language—that obligatory conceptualization, those thousands of black iron tools all interlocked for nothing, like shipwrecks, on a beach deserted for eternity—one should like to blow it all out, as the child in the tree of the universe suggests, and make of silence a path that exceeds and goes beyond all other paths! How well I understand, also, why on certain evenings I could feel the truth of negative theology!

I do understand, in fact I have never ceased to understand the words that I'd instantly wanted to think were an enigma. But equally, it is also a fact that, while understanding them, I refuse to make them mine, by which I mean I shall not invest them with an ultimate value, placed above the collision of thoughts. The intuition is a radical one, but none the truer for that. The light at the end of darkness is a temptation, but how could I forget those sleeping on the riverbank, the mark of slavery branded with red-hot iron onto their shoulder? And how could I not think of the other two, in the ancient night, who have fallen asleep, with the alarm clock soon to go off beside the bed, marking another day, largely impoverished of meaning? The mystical experience does not have the right to wipe out this feeling of sadness.

In other words? I surmise that there are two lights. The first, in the abyss of the night, for those who know how to slide into a place beyond language: starting with the whiteness of the aurora borealis, then a dazzling, and death visible, for an instant.

But how can one not love the other light, the one in which we live, light of morning and evening? Sometimes no more than a ray slanting through the clouds, sometimes the beautiful unending days of summer when the sunset seems to bring a little peace despite all reasons to feel otherwise. There are no 'golden galleons' that disappear over the horizon, but the beach is beautiful, from where one gazes at the sky, unless it be Baudelaire who comes on to the balcony with his '*chère indolente*' where they say to each other 'imperishable things' they well know to be sweet nothings, mere spume between wave and sand, a moment of happiness already reaching its end.

Two lights, two approaches to unity. The first holds that the One is not available to any formulaic thought whatsoever, so that one must abandon any hope of experiencing presence if we do not make within us a total silence, to the point even of forgetting those nearest to us. But the second would understand that what is withdrawn from words is present in the roadside flower, in the dust that the breeze raises, in the lilt of a voice, in the cries of children at play. And that it is present also in our response to words below the level of language, when it rises in us without being willed or formulated: not because the body is more than the mind, but because it is in the body where traces of what is more than formulaic thought amplify, like rings in water. The One, that absents itself infinitely from what is merely concept, is present, just as infinitely, in the humblest things presented to our vision, the humblest words simply spoken; and it can therefore dwell in satisfaction and plenitude in the most apparently modest expressions. Let us recall! '*Stanotte piove davvero*'—tonight it will rain, for sure—he exclaims, turning back towards the dark room, that the young woman that the young Leopardi, from his window on the other side of the street, hears with longing, with the need for love, which lodges in the deepest part of his being with the truth of poetry.

The One speaks through everything in existences and things, and it is not language, that sets up the obstacle, for our words possess, below the level of thought, like the earth where things can take root, the wherewithal simply to designate, let live and let flower. It is by having it close up on itself that formulation silences it. And must we not then choose like the mystic: to recognize in the light down here the shining of the One refracted by the places and the beings that vary life, that afford it the time to reveal its beauty?

De-conceptualize, so this light can grow. But such in any case is poetry's project, that remains among words because it loves things, knowing them to be the golden rain that is spread upon the speaking being, on the Danaë still in the shadow, her unity undefeated nevertheless. Strengthened by this conviction, now reaffirmed, I can now resume the task of writing which the child safe in the tree wants me to cease. This is true, and I cannot forget it: even in the most intense poems, imagination which anticipates on desire will be there to trace its own figures, and these will be conceptual once more, they will suffer loss of immediacy, be forgetful of the finite, and a black ink will spread over the light. But to desire is also to turn towards beings and things. And the dream which effaces them but that equally seeks them is not really dangerous if it knows itself to be a dream. Just as the crossing out made in writing as it progresses, may in fact be a place of sharing and exchange.

XI

But now I want to return to Genoa, which the end of my narrative scarcely seems to invite me to do, because coming out of the space in which the dream was unbroken, there was a grassy track, near a river or a stream. Genoa, that I know only slightly, moreover, because I have up to now made only two rapid visits, the second of them completely swept aside by what followed. I was to take a boat for Greece. And a few hours after the boat had left the port, it passed within hailing distance of Capraia, which was my encounter, in this world, with the island upon which—through many long summers of my life up until then—I had imagined I could locate another reality, in essence higher, because all I saw from the sea was the perfection of its rocky ridge.

That Genoa should be associated, if only by chance, with a debate between dream and reality, in no way contradicts the thought that the grassy track and the child with the fishing rod help me to sustain, to the contrary! What I have just recovered, the project for poetry, means that it is good in fact to go into the depths of words to reality as it is, removing the veil of the concept when it holds to its selection, which is to say its simplifications, its lacunae; this so often being the case with an ideology or a reverie, with Capraia having been such a one for me. And it is thus to seek to create in each life the memory of its finitude, and require of each person that he or she should love their irreducible accidence, a programme that is equally cognate with a renovation of society, because these revisions to be made, in the relationship between the individual and the self, result in a lucidity that will harden in the debate between who one is in relation to the other, and can thence dissipate some at least of the misunderstandings concerning the present moment of the being-in-the-world. From whence there comes a coagulation, as the alchemical term has it—empirical reality once more unified, and gold found at last in the hollow of language.

It is also a project, no matter how utopian, that can meld with an idea that I had of Genoa because, as I said before, of various hypotheses gleaned from the art and thought of Italy. However different at first sight Florence or Umbria, Rome or Venice seem to be, these civilizations have in common the sacrifice of what I call the dream, in order to recompose even the most immediate perceptions into a grand vision that renders them abstract, at the expense of their simple and direct quotidian. In Florence, which enacted this the first, how clear it is! Centuries had passed in which images without number had been repeated in the teaching of religion, and suddenly, it was the revival of interest in the world of Antiquity, of Greece and Rome, which returned to the foreground the things of nature in what they possess most open to life. But without delay, architects and painters imported into this approach to the world a concern with numbers, a privileging of form that decided these choices, and set the mind at a remove from ordinary existence, and so stoked the dream of a superior reality, a lucidity that would be the judge of all, which created beautiful images, but that remain images, and can do nothing therefore against the fantasies of other repressed desires, which leads to Mannerism. Florentine art has such great value, because the constraints imposed meant that great spirits inscribed their frustration, anguish and impatience into them: late Botticelli, late Michelangelo—truth laid bare, and a message for all the centuries. What remains is to set it against that intuition intrinsic to poetry.

And in Venice and Rome, this intuition has been at times more active—but there again it has been distracted by dreams, those places of power that privilege the chimeras that are born of power: over-sumptuous robes have sometimes smothered the apprehension of the simple. Piero della Francesca alone, possibly, from within the platonic or ethereal spaces managed to turn to the here and now his mastery of form and number: which he is why he is so fascinating. But, to put it briefly, the various arts are almost all under the sway of that metaphysical *imaginaire* that lays waste to many poems as well; and they incite us to think with all the more urgency of what right now we might expect from poetry, with its critique of art. Suggesting we look elsewhere, in Italy itself.

Elsewhere? Where that imagining did not wipe out memories of the finite? With this idea in mind, I used to wander, in those far-off days when I first visited Italy, into regions remote from the cities, where the ancient wisdom of peasant communities, alert to elemental things, disturb even today, or so I thought, considerations concerning pure form. But I did not thereby escape the dream, on the contrary it was a way of abandoning myself to it. I was to describe these temptations later, in a longer essay that treated of the perils and the paths of writing.[6]

And today, when I see perhaps a little clearer what writing may be, and how it is the only possible place in which to lodge a consciousness of self, how should I not find it in metaphorical form in a great port like Genoa? No trace there of those mysterious promises that seem to be held out to us in the deformation of the grand styles effected in those little chapels at the end of the track, by humble village artisans. But the vision of an activity that would resemble the true work of poetry, that tries to dismantle the dream out of loyalty—and passing underneath the formulations that saturate words—to the unending world they interpret. A great port? Boats slipping out and slipping in, fraught like poems, with goods one does not know. And those figureheads on the prow, that slide before us, with naked shoulders and grave looks, like emblematic images out of our own most archaic desires and memories. Shouts from overhead on the bridge,

6 See Bonnefoy, *The Arrière-pays*.

through the smoke. Along the dockside, sealed boxes and containers in the light that strikes everything, sometimes directly, sometimes veiled. And the whole intoxicating rocking of hulls, over deep water, and the beauty of those wood or metal curves that are what craft or industry offers as the closest approximation to the human form, while everything is in movement, in the sound of sirens, with men and women separating here, and meeting again over there. A port is in the very image of what I call writing, that activity within words that corrects dream, and continually comes up against other mirages, but undauntedly persists in seeking: seen in *contre-jour* among its signifiers, rather like masts and sails against the open sky.

Moreover, a port can be an emblem for the space and the hope of poetry when one grasps that it receives, like Genoa, a double lesson from its vast sky. On the one hand, there is what it gleans from the sunset, the hearth of dreams, and the reminder of the great longings of life. On the other hand, and more directly, the light of day: and from one season to the next, the sun either higher or lower in the sky, while inside the houses runs the almost arterial rhythm of its brilliant tracks over the dark floors of the rooms. Sometimes, in shorelines out of Claude Lorrain, when one crosses some promontory in the outskirts to the West, where the sun has already set behind the trees. But in the central foreground is the bustling, colourful and noisy scene painted by one Joseph Vernet, who had in turn read Baudelaire, summoning in lines overflowing with the fragrances of Asia and Africa, 'dazzling' dreams 'of sails, rowers, flames and masts'. I think of Genoa, am I wrong, when I hear in *La chevelure* (Head of Hair) news of a 'resounding port' where the boats

> slipping through the gold and the silk
> Open their vast arms wide to embrace the glory
> Of a pure sky quivering with the eternal heat.

A pure sky, an eternal heat. Writing as the dreamt-of release of language into the light. The memory of the evening sun to help, in words now opened to their utmost potential, bring about an acceptance of the daylight hours.

And may I say, as I close these thoughts about a narrative that was spontaneous and without preconceived intention— trusting only to the hand of night guiding the hand of day, confidently as it happens—I see no opposition between the 'grassy track' at its end, in the fading light, and the port with its abundance of more sky that was longed for almost from the first words: 'In Turin, or possibly Genoa'? Writing is this paradoxical, in fact. Where must it, disconcerted, lost among mirages and contradictions, seek to ground itself? In memories of childhood, surely, of the children that we were, in a real situation, with its worries and its sorrows. It was better for Rimbaud, after letting his imagination run wild at the beginning of *Bateau ivre*, that he should remember he had been and remained a little boy, 'full of sadness', propelling over the water of nothing more than a puddle, 'a boat as fragile as a may butterfly': precisely because it is after this decisive insight into himself that he can accede to poetry in its universal application and then write 'Royauté'.

And the child by the water's edge, 'when we went peaceably, side by side', is he not therefore, in his apparent insouciance, the first signs of a desire to write, seeking its way, and meriting thereby that I should remember him, to grasp his intuitions that later on I merely sacrificed to dreams? 'Oh, it's not about catching fish,' he told me, 'even if in those years we had little wicker baskets to put them in.' And now I remember that, yes, 'in those years', precisely, and the most clear-sighted in a lifetime, some days I would go towards the little creeks, with a fishing rod that, if it was without any kind of preparation, technique or conviction, it was because all I thought about were the 'sun fish' that lived—or so I was told, and did my cousins not catch some on occasion, but weren't they just tench?—in the swift-running waters of the Lot.

Bellies whose scales had all the colours of the sunset, or those that slide in the morning on waking, or in the long afternoons, over the flagged floors of rooms. Strange eyes that never closed because, decidedly, it was never real fish that I tried to see for so long, but those dreamt up by words. Writing can never close its hands over what would, all the same, be no more than a type of prey. But it is worth it, after all, it is worth going by the riverbank where the grass is too high, and parting it in search of a place to cast one's line.

Second Additional Note

I have reread the narrative, *Two Stages*, in the proofs of the beautiful volume that is to appear, and I reread it also when I had the pleasure of accompanying my friend Beppe Manzitti[7] in his task as translator. Which means that I had to attend carefully to phrases that I had, dare I say, merely written down. Imagine my astonishment! They appeared to me transformed, and bearing demands I never suspected simple words could have, waking and rising from the pages that contained them.

It is true that I wrote them, as I have just hinted, with my eyes closed, blindly obeying commands whose meaning I never thought to question. The strangeness of the scene that emerged—the two facing balconies in a palace courtyard, the two plays underway, identical except that one was running slightly behind the other—did not rouse me to seek any explanation. I had simply made a painting, verifying its colours and its shapes to my satisfaction, and I left it to its surface existence before me, as silent as a line can seem on a canvas.

But the difference between my original gaze, and what I saw, or rather heard, on my return! It was as if, no sooner

7 Here, Bonnefoy is referring to two of his texts: the former, *Deux scènes et notes conjointes* (Gerard Titus-Carmel illustr.) (Paris: Editions Galilée, 2009); the latter, the Italian edition of the same.

had I ceased writing it, the text began to grow restless, to exclaim, and to run over with sentences that I had thought fixed once and for all; as if, during my absence, the figures I had painted had joined together and rebelled, unable to understand my inattention when they had questions to ask me and information to provide. At which point I could not refuse the thought that I must hear them out.

This I did. Beppe Manzitte and Titus-Carmel will attest to this. When I saw a draft of the book, I realized that the addition of some supplementary text would render more harmonious its architecture, I promised that I would write an accompanying note of the required length, and set to work. Unfortunately for the book, however, I had soon written far more pages, ten times more perhaps, than what I had planned. It was no longer possible to include this overlong 'additional note' in the current elegant project. It would have to appear under a separate cover, though alongside the narrative; and to accompany this one, I had a second piece to write, which I do now.

I shall not return in the new note on what the first required of me that I should understand. This concerned aspects of my childhood, with its traumas, its astonishments, its aspirations and its anxiety. And not just my childhood but certain subsequent events of my later life, to which the writer I became had already tried to ascribe meaning. I learnt a lot, thanks to this unplanned opportunity, and I thought about it greatly, which resulted in the aforementioned essay. But following on from that sketched-out anamnesis, I see that I have two further remarks to make, one with implications that go far beyond the merely personal.

The more general remark is this: that in any existence, childhood never ends. We may well grow distant from it in time, discover places and love persons whose existence we knew nothing of and could not imagine in our earliest years, but the fact is that all this happens within a space that has been cleared by the small child we were, and the reason for this fundamental fact is simple; before what we call the age of reason, the child is able to recognize veritable presences, that may be hostile or affectionate, but always close to him, that later, with the onset of conceptual thought, the adult he will become will scarcely be able to experience, except as things. Presences? Yes, beings that are alive, with what life has of the infinite about it. And with it, by the same token, the capacity, at least sometimes, to make of them guides on the paths that open up, but that become labyrinths in the years that follow. The child had already seen what later on he will maybe recognize. He has located the house he wishes to live in, and the person he will love. We are he. The most disconcerting discoveries in *A la recherche du temps perdu* were already present behind the closed eyes of the little boy who went to bed early, carrying over into his dreams the frequently unconscious observations he had made during the day.

The other remark, this time applying to my own life but possibly of some interest to a few others beside myself, is that my own childhood did not end, and it happened very suddenly, until I discovered the vast space of Italian civilization. Did not end? No, I am not about to invalidate what I just affirmed above. Let me put it like this instead—that my childhood came to consciousness of itself in Italy, that it consented to adulthood, but at the same time without losing any of its unanswered questions, its experiences, its memory.

What strikes me, in the pages of my story, and as my first 'Additional Note' has it, is that on the one hand everything is intact from my most distant past, and on the other, the old street in the *centro storico*, the palazzo, the *cortile*, words that don't translate, and the windows that look over the courtyard with chandeliers burning behind them, the grey marker stones either side of the porches—and of course the phrase, 'Turin, perhaps, or Genoa'—would imply that we have crossed the great barrier of the Alps; everything is a memory of Italy. The river bank at the end of the narrative, with its tall grass where the pre-teen wanders with his fishing rod—that is certainly in France, the Loire or the Lot of my earliest years. But the Genovese palace is just besides my traveller, at any instant I can return there, and if I start writing again, perhaps I shall end up there: the French past and the Italian present exist as one in my reverie and in my life, and I can explain why.

For childhood, as I have suggested, is the time when real presences speak, and they habituate us to hearing what, as such, they say—something we never entirely stop doing— even if we allow ourselves to get taken over by what we call the unconscious. And Italy is the country where, drawing on the source of the ancient world, which was similarly haunted, great artists conceived works that posed the question of presence, integrating it in statues, in paintings and frescoes, among which it is only natural therefore to enquire, if one remembers, and, literally, to be reborn. As I write these words, I turn back to the years when my first way of living in the world had come to an end. Until that time I had studied with my head down, while listening almost instinctively to the sounds that reached me from poetry. But in the matter of painting, architecture and music I had not yet made any decisive choices, as if I were crossing a long period of latency, recognized as such, when I first set foot on the soil of Provence or Corsica, and then Italy. Alberti or Piero della Francesca, to whom I frequently refer compulsively, instantly swept away my vague and dissatisfied interest in Surrealist painting, even when they were reminiscent of some of De Chirico's early work. After which my research into great Tuscan, Roman and also Venetian art was ceaselessly bound up with my more directly poetic writing.

This is what *Two Stages* taught me, or helped me to understand. But I have a further remark to make, for I have not forgotten the discoveries that this narrative opened up to me, and that it took me two attempts to understand. The thoughts that became clear were already within me, the written text assures me of that, where they are in fact carefully deposited in metaphors or other figures, but I did not listen to what was being said to me there, I put it off until some time 'later', which risked becoming 'never': whereupon the agitation in my text. What might a clarification like this, achieved in two parts mean? Does it not contain a further message? Less, this time, concerned with the return of events or emotions from a remote or even recent past, so much as an explanation of the somnambulism that affects certain moments of writing?

I believe that there is, and this is how I have come to formulate it. Writing is not a simple act, or to be more precise, the act of a person in any sense simple. We are all Janus-faced, and the erosion of that stone mask reveals the effect of time, which also wears out our lives. Within us there is someone watching, who possesses a certain knowledge and who meditates on it, embodying it when the opportunity arises in its own language, often in a text, or a painting, but we are also the person who refuses that kind of knowledge, and who closes his eyes, within the text or the image itself.

That knower is 'the deep I'—*le Je profond*—that Rimbaud called 'an other'; it is in the child's gaze where it lives among the presences: he had received the keys to remembering and understanding and he never stops doing so. Whereas the person who does not want to know, or the one who at least defers thought of it, is the ego that we become in later life, forgetful of our origin; or rather it could be the artist at the heart of that ego, the artist that frequents the desires that make up this later life, among realities that have become things to be possessed, and who puts his mastery of forms at the service of this desire for possession, of this dream. Form is in effect perfect for dreaming, because a form emerges out of an excess of matter, which entails, when applied to a life, the elimination of facts up against which it meets the constraints that would forbid the dream. True, this can be the case—and then we get great art, whether in writing, painting, music or architecture—a way of working on the relationship to the self, to release the essential, and to transmute it into wisdom. But it is also, most often, that which cuts into lived experience to release something that enables us to forget the finite: a forgetfulness often taken for beauty.

And poetry, well, poetry is the persistence with which the vigilance of 'the deep I' surveys the intentions of the ego, and animates its huge potential in form; but in effective writing the ego is not without its seductions and powers, its ploy being to distract he who has written from what he will go on to write, absorbing him in the ways he might create work more easily, and of the surface, in obedience to his dreams whether ordinary or sublimated: in such a way that the opportunities to take stock get lost. But time never stops moving on, nor age increasing, and this incites the writer to look back, and to verify whether or not in his pages, he has deprived himself of what could have or might still give some meaning to his life.

I am given to thinking, today, that the few months which elapsed between the composition of my narrative and the day the first draft of the book arrived, was more than enough for me to take stock of time passing, and to be alarmed: because it was then that I returned to what I had written but had not understood, forcing myself to listen properly this time, and even believing, whether it be true or not, that in some measure I did so.

In December 2015, six months before his death at the age of 93, Yves Bonnefoy concluded what was to be his last major text in prose, *L'Echarpe rouge*. To that final page, he appended two sets of dates, 1964–2015, followed by 'Juin–décembre 2015'. For *L'Echarpe rouge*, as he explains in detail at the opening of the book, began as an enigmatic series of poetic fragments, written in 1964 under some compulsion, that try as he might, the poet could neither change nor add to in any way that satisfied him. Another text from 2015, this time a long poem, *Ensemble encore*, may be considered his last work in verse. Both works have about them an aura of valediction, especially the poem, which is an address to past Masters, a summoning of memories and a restatement of his poetic mission, ending on a radiant image of his loved ones, a woman and a child, caught laughing in the sudden onset of summer rain. A recording of the poem, made by the poet before his death, was played at his funeral on 11 July 2016 in the Columbarium at Père Lachaise, before assembled mourners, his friends, who were thus addressed a final time by the poet's voice.

Of these two late writings, *Ensemble encore* was translated as *Together Still* by Hoyt Rogers and published by Seagull Books in 2017; it fell to me to translate the longer prose text, to which I shall refer to from now as *The Red Scarf*. The original French edition, published by Mercure de France, contained in addition to the principal text, three earlier writings with important thematic links to the major 'anamnesis', or act of remembrance: *Two Stages*, written in April 2008, which is a short dream narrative, as well as two exegeses of that narrative, one of them, 'An Aid to Understanding' being of considerable length and complexity. The Mercure edition gathered these four texts, which were then republished by Gallimard in their *Collection Folio* in December 2017. It is clear therefore that the poet wished the main text, *The Red Scarf*, to be published in association with the other three, and this has been respected in the present translation.

*

The Red Scarf is described by Yves Bonnefoy as an 'anamnesis', which I assume is a reference to the word's Greek etymology, meaning an act of remembrance, although there is also a specifically Christian liturgical sense of the word, concerning Christ's words at the Last Supper. There is indeed a sense in this text of a rite being observed, not religious, but rather a filial act of piety involving a recognition of loss and possibly neglect, followed by an earnest attempt to make, however belatedly, amends, and to achieve some measure of reconciliation. Early on in the book, the poet sets down the matter succinctly: 'My most troubling memory, when I was between ten and twelve years old, concerns my father, and my anxiety about his silence'. There follows an extraordinary, and very moving, anatomy of his father's silence, and the melancholy that seemed to take hold some years in to his marriage. For at the heart of the book is the ballad of Elie and Hélène, the poet's parents, the story of their lives together and their changing relationship, seen through the eyes of their son— the boy's intense, yet inchoate experience, reviewed through the eyes of the now-elderly man.

'Ah memories, memories, what would you have with me, at this moment of my life?' the narrator exclaims in the older dream narrative *Two Stages*. *The Red Scarf* is indeed an act of memory, a deliberate attempt to redeem the time. The word 'memoir' seems too flimsy to describe it; it is an autobiography, but it is more than that. Like his earlier 'excited reverie' from 1972, *The Arrière-pays*, it is part autobiography, part spiritual and intellectual history, and part a poet's credo. I wrote of Bonnefoy's aim in the introduction to my translation of the above-mentioned work: 'with rare intellectual and emotional discipline, the poet clearly set himself the task of anatomizing his spiritual trajectory up to that point, following the river back to its source in the intensities of his often solitary childhood.'[1] Bonnefoy completed this earlier text in 1972, on the eve of his fiftieth year; it is moving to consider that the poet made the same effort at summation over forty years later in *The Red Scarf*, written when he was in his nineties. Although there is a wealth of published prose and poetry in between, the two volumes are in a sense companion

1 Bonnefoy, *The Arrière-pays*, p. 3.

pieces; for example, the fourth chapter of *The Arrière-pays* evokes his childhood years, divided between the *grisaille* of working life in the poorer quarters of Tours, and the idyllic summers spent in the south, at the home of his maternal grandparents in the village of Toirac on the Lot; this material is vastly amplified in *The Red Scarf* to include detailed elements of geography and social history; the exact origins and status of his parents being essential to the poet's theme.

This is not the place to rehearse Bonnefoy's poetics in any detail; they have been analysed in depth by others on numerous occasions, and by myself in the introduction to *The Arrière-pays* mentioned above.[2] It would be superfluous too, given that the poet refers to his final book as being itself an exegesis. His first and last intention here is to decipher and draw out the meanings concealed in the fragments he wrote down in 1964—the book is an impassioned and at times quite heady interpretation of signs and enigmas. Working so to speak against the clock, the urge to understand is by the end extraordinarily fruitful; the reader can only look on in amazement as line after line yields up its psychological and textual pith. Sometimes, notably in the cerebral 'explanatory' text, 'An Aid To Understanding', hermeneutic links and solutions are established with breathtaking certainty; and in the principal text the metaphoric

2 See, for example, John Naughton's 'Introduction' to a recent selection of Bonnefoy's poems: Yves Bonnefoy, *Poems* (Anthony Rudolf, John Naughton and Stephen Romer eds) (Manchester: Carcanet Press, 2017) pp. *xiii–xlvii*.

transformation undergone by the red scarf itself, initially laid over the shoulders and chest of the unknown man, and then the poet's own, is an almost baroque progression from filial bond to maternal blood—as when the young Hélène offers the 'scarf' to her future husband, and hidden within the gift is the blood link to come, with the son. When revelation of this nature is at the flood, *procul, o procul este, profani.*

*

That said, as a long-time student of Bonnefoy's *oeuvre* I thought it might be helpful to pinpoint certain continuities and new departures, repetitions and fresh emphases, as they occur in these final writings. What is immediately striking, obviously, is the highly personal nature of *The Red Scarf*. It is as if, at this late stage of his life, Bonnefoy relaxes his own severe rule of impersonality; the earlier work reflects the life, undoubtedly, but transformed, elevated, mythologized. Anecdotal and circumstantial material is mostly burnt away. It was, however, present in *The Arrière-pays*, as we have seen, and then, in a remarkable departure, there were the poems about 'la maison natale' ('The House where I was born') in Tours, and about his parents, in *Les Planches courbes* (The Curved Planks, 2001). The child's vision, understood as a pre-conceptual, non-taxonomic *imaginaire*, has always been central to Bonnefoy's poetics of presence, and he has been able, apparently at will, to dip into the reservoir of childhood memory. But whereas the relation with his mother has been the veritable source (the passages in *The Red Scarf* about his mother Hélène teaching him to read as a boy, sharing with him the simple words and images from an illustrated ABC primer could not make the matter clearer), the obscurely thwarted relation with his father, which is the creative anxiety at the heart of the book, had always been a matter to be approached, if at all, then with immense caution and *pudeur*. The matter is broached, however, movingly and haltingly, in *Les Planches courbes*, and in a series of irregular sonnets called *Raturer outre* from 2009, the same year he wrote *Two Stages and Additional Notes*, though Bonnefoy makes no mention of the poems in the opening to *The Red Scarf*. A great deal is present there in embryo however: an allusion to the Max Ernst painting *La Révolution la nuit*, with its opening quote from Freud[3] '*Père, ne vois-tu pas que je brûle?*'; a poem entitled 'L'Echarpe rouge' and another called 'L'Idée d'un livre' in which a child addresses his father, '*Ah, ouvrier*'—ah, worker—and invites him, in a haunting image, to go ' "limping" together into the future'.

The relation with the father is something hidden, but momentous: the title *Raturer outre* has been explained by Bonnefoy as a way of using form—the loose sonnet—as a passive producer of content, such that without form, which both constrains and produces: 'I would not have known what

---

3 'Father, don't you see I'm burning?' See *The Present Hour* (Beverley Bie Brahic trans.) (London: Seagull Books, 2013), especially the sequence 'Strike Further' (pp. 9–31).

someone inside me had to tell me'.[4] The need to repress the painful memory is revealed, famously, in the seventh poem from the earlier sequence 'Dans la maison natale', when one Sunday afternoon, over a game of cards, profiting from his momentary absence, the child replaces his father's cards with a winning hand, so 'Now the loser would win', and the child might provide the father with 'some kind of hope'. The section ends with this confession:

> I've crossed these words out everywhere
> A hundred times, in verse, in prose,
> But I cannot: always they well up again,
> And tell their truth.)[5]

While in the poems biographical identity is never explicit (though strongly implied), there is still a mythological substratum; in the prose narrative of *The Red Scarf*, this is allowed to fall away, and the early descriptions of his parents, their social origins and their meeting, constitutes, apart from anything else, a remarkable extended piece of social history, unparalleled in the poet's work. Mythology is still there, but as an incidental emphasis rather than structuring element. When he does 'mythologize' it is unforgettable: having spoken of the reading lessons he received from Hélène, she is described, in a vignette that must rank high in the annals

4 Quoted in Bonnefoy, *The Present Hour*, p. 100.
5 See Bonnefoy, *Poems*, p. 222.

of a son's adoration for his mother, as 'this gatherer-together of a world coming apart, this Isis of the little house by the railway line' (p. 84). If the poet's father, Élie, does not receive equivalent elevation, *The Red Scarf* moves with compassion around his shade, and the poet writes one of his finest sentences, remembering the straitened, unhappy circumstances within which his parents spent so much of their lives: 'The mystical experience does not have the right to wipe out this feeling of sadness' (p. 185).

*

After the filial relationships, all-important in *The Red Scarf*, comes the natural imagery, the landscapes of the Auvergne and the Lot, of the rough *Causse*, or upper ridge-land and the garden with fruit trees below; and then there is the uninterpreted dream imagery, which wells up continuously in Bonnefoy's *oeuvre*—not just the ideal but inaccessible country of the *Arrière-pays* but the dark canal with heaps of coal, the iron bridge and the pool of oil, the tree on the hill, the place of rough grasses, the swollen river with boats upon it and possibly no place to land on the far side. These recurrent images that emerge apparently unmediated from the poet's unconscious are not 'explained' in Bonnefoy's final prose work, but they are revisited and given context. Such experiences, to which the poet here gives the term '*surgissement*'— by which he means that an object instantaneously becomes detached from its surroundings and 'stands forth'—existed, as he says, 'in the here and now, where I was, and not yet where words called to me, beyond the horizon of the known world' (p. 90). In *The Red Scarf* there is one image in particular, or one *surgissement*, of a 'black silhouette against the light, a man standing, bent over some task or other (. . .)', and the young Bonnefoy, who sees this man, framed in his window at Toirac one night as darkness comes on, experiences, 'in this standing forth, which is nothing else, in and of itself, than total solitude, an infinite vulnerability' (p. 92).

I think the vertigo, even the terror, of non-being, the experience of what Eliot called in a different context 'vastation'— both a spiritual spoliation and a spiritual purging— is vital to understanding Bonnefoy's later insistence (and that is the right word) that poetry should always, finally, be affirmative—of presence, but also accepting of mortal change ('finitude'), and should celebrate the humblest, but most ancient elements like rock and stone. The affirmative nature of his poetics, which can seem at times prescriptive—in *The Red Scarf*, after all, three considerable poets are taken to task: Eliot for a failure of hope, Valéry for a failure of seriousness, Pierre Jean Jouve for a failure of theme—must I think have its origin in this early, vertiginous experience of the void. One might add that the three poets named had if not identical, then similar such experiences. Another contributing factor must be Bonnefoy's acute sense of the critical, 'terrorist' age in which he lived, the 'age of suspicion' and the 'linguistic turn', in which poetry, and subjective, lyrical expression in general, was under attack; he was thus on a rescue mission, stated as early as 1959: 'I would like to bring together, almost identify, poetry and hope'.[6]

*

There is one final image I should like to evoke, if I might be permitted a personal favourite. It occurs in the original 1964 fragment, where the narrator recounts a visit he makes:

> I remembered the village near Toulouse,
> And the house of the young painter
> Who I knew then, briefly,
> Then he died. An old house
> With deep recessed windows,
> With whitewashed walls. And I had drunk
> Eagerly at that cup of whiteness,
> I who came from the poor rooms
> With their flowery wallpaper.

The '*papier à fleurs des chambres pauvres*', the flowery wallpaper, recurs several times in Bonnefoy's work, notably in his description of the house in Tours, in *The Arrière-pays*, which is also associated with a 'penury of images': and so it is that one experience of a heaven opening up, a *surgissement*, but of a joyous kind, would be a bare whitewashed wall and, since this is the home of a painter, a white wall with a painting

6 Quoted in Bonnefoy, *Poems*, p. *xlvii*.

hanging on it. This whiteness, from which the thirsty visitor drinks so eagerly, reminds me of the poet's words on first visiting Italy, some years later: 'I visited the churches and the museums and saw on all those white walls the Madonnas of Giotto and Masaccio and Piero, grave, serene, almost standing free in their flawless presence'.[7] It also looks forward to his discovery of the former monastic building in Valsaintes, Haute-Provence, where he and his wife Lucie spent many summers in the vast, whitewashed, half-ruined rooms, and where he wrote some of his greatest poetry. We are given here an authentic link, from one moment in the poet's intense mental and sensuous experience to another; from a house near Toulouse to the churches and museums of Italy, and on to Valsaintes. It is the achievement of *The Red Scarf*, the final, retrospective prose work of this Master, to light up facets and fragments of the work, all the way back to where it began.

*

As far as the translation is concerned, the difficulties associated with 'Englishing' Bonnefoy—and we are many to have encountered them—appear on cue. It is generally agreed now that two key terms, *présence* and *finitude* are to be simply reproduced *per se*, in their English versions, since they have accrued such contextual weight they have become talismanic. *The Red Scarf*, incidentally, contains paragraphs that might usefully define both these terms. The word *imaginaire* I have

7 See Bonnefoy, *The Arrière-pays*, p. 67.

kept in French, since no English formulation quite covers its meaning, the free-floating hedonistic pool of signifiers, that in Lacan precedes the phase of the *symbolique* in the infant's apprehension of the world. Occasionally, I have translated a word, and then indicated its French original, where a particular difficulty or a new usage is implied, as for example with the word '*surgissement*'.

*

It remains for me to thank various people: my publisher, Naveen Kishore, of Seagull Books, for his continued vision, enthusiasm, generosity of spirit and patience; my fellow *bonnefidéliens et amis de longue date*, John Naughton and Anthony Rudolf; my friends and colleagues at Tours and Oxford, who have given me occasion to speak on Bonnefoy.

Above all I am grateful, and honoured, that Yves Bonnefoy should have entrusted the translation of this work to me. I hope I have not betrayed that trust. He was anxious that the book should appear in English, which is the native language of his widow, Lucie. The poet dedicated this work to his daughter Mathilde, and my deep gratitude goes also to her, for her trust, encouragement and *bienveillance* throughout.

Stephen Romer
Le Clos Châalis,
Touraine, January 2019